MIRROR ON

C000078857

Want some psychic insight into yo
Maybe even contact a loved one ... ...

Then Nathen Turner is the man, a renowned psychic medium offering comfort and closure to his loyal clients. The only problem is, he's a fake – a smooth-talking con man with a briefcase full of conjuring tricks.

From tarot cards to séances, *Mirror on the Soul,* is an entertaining journey into the world of fraudsters and the supernatural.

'Atmospheric and entertaining thriller, told with style and humour'
Karol Griffiths, Hollywood Script Editor

MIRROR ON THE SOUL

Andrew Langley

Cover image used under licence from Shutterstock.com
Typeset in Minion Pro

British Library Cataloguing in Publication Data.
A catalogue record for this book
is available from the British Library.

ISBN 978-0-9554137-1-1

Published by LPS Creative Media
www.lpscreativemedia.com

AUTHOR'S NOTE

This novel is a work of fiction. Names, characters, places
and incidents are either the product of the author's
imagination or are used fictionally. Any resemblance
to actual events, locales or persons, living or dead,
is entirely coincidental.

To discover more about the Nathen Turner novels,
and read news, views and extracts visit:

www.andrewlangley.co.uk

DEDICATION

For my mother and father. Forever missed.

CHAPTER 1

THE PSYCHIC MEDIUM

At the casino in Las Vegas, Nathen Turner's game was deception. Press a few hundred dollars into his crooked palm and he'd pretend to talk to the dead or see into the future. As a fraudulent psychic medium he preyed on grief, like some sort of spiritual parasite for the bereaved and vulnerable. Now in Vegas for the third time he was on the hunt for more eager victims in need of his particular brand of comfort and closure.

The sense of sheer desperation on the casino floor that morning was overwhelming. Even the oxygen-enriched air-conditioning was struggling to clear the heady mix of stale cologne and nervous perspiration that permeated the room. Row upon row of clinking and churning slot machines bleeped and chimed their congratulations every time somebody won ten cents. The human robots that stoked the spinning wheels seemed completely unaware that they had spent twenty dollars to get the ten cents.

Turner watched with amusement an elderly lady eagerly feeding shiny brass tokens into a small chrome slot before desperately yanking down the smooth steel bar that spun the reels. She sat back glassy-eyed on her stool, exhausted from the effort. Lemon, pear, cherry – nothing this time – feed the machine – cherry, pear, cherry – nothing again. On and on it went, line upon line of twitching humanity, their efforts filling the room with so much mechanical noise it was like living inside a gigantic clock.

At this early hour there was little action on the blackjack, roulette and craps tables so the machines were providing a vital gambling fix to the restless masses. Judging by the wrinkled clothes and funky smells, many had been playing them for hours, only breaking off to go to the bathroom with a polite 'Can you watch my machine for me' to one of the black-shirted floor attendants.

Turner could never really understand the attraction of Vegas and its twinkling twenty-four hours a day lifestyle. Yes, the food was amazing and the rooms weren't expensive, but, man, it was hot. Step outside the casinos or shopping malls and you were hit by a blast of scorching air like you'd walked into hell itself. Billed as an adult playground to meet any human desire, prostitution was actually illegal within the city limits. This didn't stop talented ladies of the night slipping fifty dollars to casino security so they could hang out at the sports bars, fishing for clientele. A quick shimmy up to a likely target, and an 'accidental' shove followed by a profuse apology – this was the normal method of breaking the ice. Then a sexy smile and husky 'May I sit here? My name's Amy. What's yours?' Night after night, Turner witnessed the spectacle unfold. He could sense the guy's internal conflicted dialogue – 'What will the wife say, does she look clean, man, she's hot, I wonder how much, what will she do?' – followed by a guilty submission and trip to his room for a full ten minutes of carnal bliss. He often wondered whether the marketing slogan 'What happens in Vegas stays in Vegas' rang true. He hoped so for the sake of all the marriages and trusting relationships it had jeopardised over the years.

What he adored about Vegas was that nobody gave a damn what you looked like. His appearance often drew amazed looks and mutterings back home in the UK, but here he was just one of the colourful crowd. At a slim six feet three inches, he wasn't easy to miss. His loud blue Hawaiian shirt, denim jeans, cowboy boots and black concho belt fitted right in. A mess of unkempt shoulder-length blonde hair completed the look that made him appear to be a weird love child of the Wild West and beach culture. Turner was comfortable that way and he liked it.

Slowly, he glided his way down past the noisy casino machines and stepped blissfully into the relative calm of the wide corridor that sloped down to the attached conference centre. Through the doors on his right, he could see the large outdoor pool where beautiful beach bodies were already out in force, toasting each other in the desert heat. The decoration was what he called 'shabby chic'. Cheap herringbone red carpet with cream side stripes and the odd fake marble figurine firmly screwed to the wall, watching blindly as you went by. Thankfully, the musk of the casino floor had given way to the smell of flower-scented air freshener, and he gratefully inhaled the sweet aroma. Generic background music washed through the passageway, accompanying his strides like some bizarre slow marching band.

Finally, after ten minutes of carefully weaving his way past the crowds at the cheap side stalls offering cold junk food and a programme for 'only' twenty-five dollars, he found what he was looking for. Signs above his head read, 'Psychic Fair This Way – Main Conference Centre', in bold yellow curly type on a glossy purple background bursting with white stars. He lifted the laminated lanyard around his neck to the waiting conference receptionist blocking his path. After glancing carefully at the identity photograph and typescript title, 'Nathen Turner, Psychic Medium, UK', she ushered him past with the obligatory 'Have a nice day'. Turner had been networking at the fair for the last three days, trying to build contacts in the States with little luck. As an unknown spiritual worker from out of town, with no TV or media exposure in the US, he was politely ignored by most. He'd finally caught a break yesterday when the local news crew had inadvertently stopped him, amongst many others, for vox pop style quotes about the conference. They liked his quirky British accent so his brief thirty-second interview had appeared on the local news last night. Now he was a man in demand, and he loved it.

Encouraged by his raised profile he had hired a room behind the main hall and confirmed bookings for two private psychic readings already. As he approached, he could see his first lady anxiously waiting for him at the door. She gave him a nervous smile and reached out her manicured hand towards him.

'Hello, I'm Nathen Turner. It's a pleasure to meet you. Sorry to keep you waiting.' He found that being slightly camp in his speech and mannerisms made his female clientele feel more comfortable. Assuming he was gay seemed to make them relax more and not feel like he was hitting on them. His quick top-to-toe scan of her from the doorway had already told him she was having relationship issues with her husband, and from the white tan line on her left third finger he could tell that her wedding band had been recently removed. Or maybe she was divorced; either way something had gone wrong. Her clothes were well tailored in shades of red with matching shoes and a handbag. The red was making a statement – she was power dressing and needed to feel important. Carelessly manicured hands painted with red nail varnish the same shade as the dress completed the look. She seemed worried and nervous, but her bearing was proud – at one time she had been someone people looked up to with respect. The whole impression created an aura of a neat, organised professional person, possibly a Virgo, he thought to himself. Virgos were notoriously detail orientated but that didn't fit with her shabby nail polish. The shade was an exact match for her clothing – maybe she had some sort of emotional turmoil that could explain the lack of care in its application. Guessing star signs was just part of his stock in trade, and over the years he'd developed almost a sixth sense for them.

All this sped through his mind as he reached out to accept the offered hand, shook it warmly and gently led her into the room. Purple velvet drapes lined the walls, giving the setting a suitably spiritual feel, with a small circular card table in the centre accompanied by two high-backed ornate chairs. Pulling back a chair, he gestured her to sit down.

'It is important you say as little as possible right now – I don't want you thinking you have somehow given me clues to what ails you. We must trust in the spirits to guide us.' Turner's standard opening line always worked and helped the more sceptical client relax.

He removed a small battered brown leather Gladstone briefcase from behind one of the drapes and set it carefully onto the centre of the green baize of the card table. Theatrically opening the two brass clasps, he gently removed a deck of tarot cards as if holding a newborn baby. This was all part of the show and helped build an air of mystery around the whole choreographed procedure, one he had done profitably thousands of times before. The cards were shrouded in a decorative purple silk with an abalone shell clasp holding the fabric in place. He delicately unfolded the thin material, as if the contents were the most fragile substance known to man, and laid it out flat and square in the middle of the table. Very faint alchemical symbols covered the cloth and it looked old but well preserved. Next he placed the large tarot cards, with a half-chequerboard half-red back design, in the exact centre of the silky cloth. The deck was only about ten years old, but he had carefully sprayed each card with a thin coat of brown enamel paint, sanded them, then gently bent and dog-eared the corners, so they looked much more ancient. Old meant revered in the psychic world, and he went to great lengths to make sure his props fit that bill. Finally, he removed a thick white church candle and a small brown clipboard, complete with notepaper and a short yellow pencil.

'Before we begin I'd just like you to close your eyes and take a few deep breaths to calm your thoughts.' He quietly eased himself into the chair opposite, lighting the candle and using the time for a closer physical inspection of his client. She had placed her small handbag on the floor and he could see inside it. A bottle of Vicodin, the strong narcotic pain medication, rested beside a neatly folded handkerchief centrally tucked in a side pocket. More attention to detail, he thought, considering the deliberate way the white fabric had been placed. Now he felt more confident in his astrological assessment. She was Virgo through and through.

'Do you feel relaxed and ready to connect and seek guidance from the spirits?' She simply nodded in reply. 'Please pick up the clipboard and write down the one key question or issue you would like us to resolve today. Once you have done this please rip off the piece of paper and fold it tightly.' As she did, he got up and moved to the other side of the room as if adjusting the purple drapes. Subconsciously it signalled to her that there was no way he could read what she had written.

'We will burn this as an offering to the spirits,' he said, and in one movement he swept it from her hand into the candle. A huge jet of flame shot up into the air as the paper flared and instantly disappeared. It was a chemically treated paper used in theatres to create an instant flash effect. She jumped and gasped in astonishment. Under this misdirection, he casually picked up the clipboard, opened a hidden magnetic back panel and read the impression her writing had left behind. The clever construction of this simple conjuring device made its secret undetectable, and, as it was his own design, he was immensely proud of it. Quickly he flipped the hidden panel closed again. From her point of view, she had written a personal note and burnt it and he had no idea what it contained. But he knew she had written, 'Will my husband Bobby ever come back to me now I'm sick?'

Now he had all the information he needed for his reading. The rest was just putting on a convincing performance, playing the role of a caring person bringing closure and hope to his clientele. 'Please take the cards and mix them until you feel a connection. You will know when this happens – you will feel it. Now cut them once with your left hand and place them back on the table.' Cautiously at first she picked them up, as if handling a revered religious artefact, then mixed them slowly on her lap. Cutting with her left hand felt awkward, but she was totally convinced that this was an essential part of the ritual.

Reaching over he took the top card and placed it face down to her left. 'This card represents your past.' The second card he placed in the centre. 'This card represents your present situation.' And finally he placed the third card to the right. 'This last one is your future.' Turner knew exactly which card was in which position as he could read the small identifying markings he'd made on the back of them. Now all he had to do was weave a story around the card illustrations that fit with his earlier guesswork and observations.

The first card, the one on her left representing the past, was 'The Empress' and he gave her time to look at the illustration after he deftly turned it face up. The picture showed a naked lady with a crown on her head, leaning calmly against a tree with a young blonde-haired child at her feet. They appeared to be in a coastal setting and surrounded by the bounty of nature, with purple and yellow flowers cascading across the landscape. An orange tree towered over the nude, weighed down with its bulging fruit.

'This card represents your past and shows how you enjoyed good health, not just physical but in your relationships as well. Also in the past you never had to worry about money, represented here by the bounty of plants in their surroundings. The outdoor setting suggests you are more an outdoor person and don't like being cooped up inside buildings. People who present this card are usually from the star sign Virgo with the

Empress representing the purity of the virgin. Certainly in the past you were very organised and everything seemed to be on track.'

During the monologue Turner didn't bother to look up; he guessed at least eighty per cent of what he had said was right from his previous visual analysis of her and his educated guess about her star sign. The 'being outdoors' was a hunch based on the depth of her tan. From her point of view, his fixed gaze on the card only added to her sense of awe at what he had said. He had her undivided attention as he gently flipped over the centre card – the 'Knight of Swords'. The card showed a knight in plate armour astride a huge purple lizard. The knight held a silver sword with a green handle in his right hand and a shield emblazoned with the motif of a lion's head in his left. The lizard was turning its head angrily as if to strike, but no wounds were shown on either figure.

'This card represents your present day and tells me you are in a conflict of some sort. Usually it means problems in a close relationship that has led to trauma and created a lot of difficulties in the family. The knight's armour, although plate, is plain and certainly not luxurious, suggesting that money, or lack of it, may have become an issue. The creature can mean illness or a severe change in circumstances you have to battle with. Although it is affecting you, nothing is showing yet to the outside world. Your outer 'armour' is unmarked just as the knight shown on the card. The lion on the shield tells me that whatever the issues are, you are facing them with courage. However, there will be very difficult times ahead and important decisions to make.'

Turner based this on spotting the bottle of pain pills and

the missing wedding band. He couldn't see anything physically wrong with her, hence the suggestion she was covering up her issues. She began to sob and reached down to lift the small lace handkerchief from her bag.

'Please … please, go on. Tell me what you see in the future.' Her mascara had smeared across her upper cheek and her eyes were red.

He knew he had her now and there was no escape. She would want to know more and more and would be eternally grateful to him for essentially telling her what she already knew. Without hesitation he reached over and flipped the third card, 'The Star'. In the centre of the image sat a beautiful mermaid with blonde hair and a sweeping green fish tale. A golden crown sat centrally on the mermaid's head, and above her six stars with a sun and moon circled the sky with a white dove on the right. Both her breasts were naked. From her left breast poured a red liquid and from her right a white one, both emptying into the rippling ocean below.

'This card illustrates your future and shows a return to the calm and balance you once enjoyed, with the heavens again surrounding you and guiding you on your way. The poison you feel in your life right now is being poured away and replaced with peace, just like the dove of peace on the card, flying in to watch over you. All trouble will pass, and you will find yourself content and happy in time.'

Clients always liked a happy ending, and when he finally looked up she was smiling amidst the tears. She stared fixedly at the naked breasts of the mermaid on the card.

'I have breast cancer – it's like the cards know. See the red pouring from her chest … I don't know what to say … how could this be possible? They gave me drugs for pain but to be honest it doesn't actually hurt at all.' Her amazed gaze was scanning the cards, totally in awe of this demonstration of psychic ability.

Weird coincidences like this were always happening to him in readings. It felt like the spirit world delighted in throwing him the odd curve ball. The only problem was, he didn't believe in the supernatural any more. When his father died of a heart attack shortly after his forty-seventh birthday, he'd spent years trying every spiritual ritual he knew to contact him. Nothing had worked, and it left him bitter and disillusioned with the whole psychic scene. Now he relied solely on his wits and intuition and put down the odd coincidence to luck rather than any mystical help.

Turner needed to buy some time to think about how he should handle the new information about her cancer. Here was a real opportunity for him to make some serious money. His mind flashed back to her written message on the piece of paper.

'Who is Bobby,' he said quickly, 'and why do I see him walking away with his back to you?'

She jumped in surprise. 'Bobby is my husband … he walked out on me two weeks ago. He said he just couldn't cope with the cancer, working full time and looking after our teenage kids.'

'I can see you face some difficult decisions. Perhaps we can do a deeper reading to help guide you. It is more expensive I'm afraid …' he said, just letting the statement hang in the air as he watched her reaction carefully.

Throwing a fistful of bills onto the table she pleaded,

'Please help me; I don't know what to do. Is that enough?'

Without wanting to look too eager, Turner reached out for the money and placed his hand gently on hers. 'I'm sure it will be. Please just relax and let us seek further guidance from the spirits.'

Now he knew she had more than one child and they were both teenagers. Also her husband worked and was probably busy away from home most days. He could play with this to dig deeper and change his guesswork into cast-iron certainties. As he continued with a range of more complicated card spreads including the Celtic Cross, she was positively buzzing, smiling and nodding at everything he said. After another hour he brought the reading to a close. Reaching over, she put her hand gently on his.

'Thanks. That has really helped me see things more clearly. I have hope now … you've helped give me my life back.' Another satisfied customer, he thought silently to himself, delighting in the feel of the wad of notes in his pocket.

'Thank you. It's been my pleasure. I'm blessed to have met you today and I wish you the best. May your God go with you.' And with that he led her slowly out into the corridor, holding her hand in his. She hugged him warmly, and he watched as she smiled and waved back at him through the crowd still jostling outside the conference hall.

When he headed back into the room his second client was already inside sitting at the small card table, irritatingly rapping her fingers on the soft green surface. She was an attractive mid-thirties brunette dressed more for the gym than an afternoon out.

'Hi, I'm Nathen Turner. Nice to meet you. I see you've

found your way in OK. May I offer you a water?'

The brunette shook her pretty head and scowled. 'Look I've been waiting over half an hour outside, and if we don't get a move-on I'm going to be late for my aerobics class. Get rid of those stupid cards and candle. I'm not into mumbo jumbo crap, OK? If you can really speak to the dead like you said on TV, what the hell do you need those for?' She folded her arms tightly across her chest and glared at him.

'Have you ever been to a medium before?' The words were spoken softly to counter her abrupt manner.

'Nope and probably never will again if all you do is a load of card tricks and spooky shit,' she replied, her arms clenching tighter to her body, her posture bolt upright, challenging him.

Moving gently into the chair opposite, he smiled at her, trying to lighten the mood. This was one bitter lady who acted like she was at war with the world. Turner needed to slow things down and get her to relax.

'There is a lot of spiritual energy around you,' he said, closing his eyes briefly for effect. 'I just like the spirits to talk to me about things first. Most of the time they will bring up and talk about everything that you would like to, or perhaps more importantly need to hear.'

Continuing to speak gently and calmly, he pushed the cards and candle off the table out of sight. Reaching around to his rear jeans hip pocket, he pulled out a small red notebook, laid it open in front of him and picked up the pencil from the clipboard. Slowly he began to sketch wide uneven circles on the blank pages. This drew her gaze and for the first time it allowed him to get a good look at her. To his complete disappointment there was very little to see. No handbag, no cosmetic jewellery and no real clue from her black Lycra jogging pants or plain orange T-shirt. The only thing of note was that she had a man's plain gold wedding ring on her ring finger. This stood out to him as unusual given the rest of her very drab appearance.

'I always feel a reading is what we need rather than what we want,' he continued, and as he spoke he wrote 'THE RING' in block capitals inside one of the circles. 'I feel the spirit is interrupting my speech. I don't know whom I'm talking to; I just feel this tremendous amount of love. Almost like it's the love of my life ...'

She jolted upright, staring at the pad. 'What did you write there? Oh my God, it's real! I wore my husband's wedding ring today ... just thinking if it was him ... he would know and send me a sign. Oh my God!' Her speech came between huge gulps of air as she struggled for breath.

So now he knew her husband was dead. She wasn't that old so he must have died young, which usually meant either an accident or some form of critical illness. Using the information he continued calmly.

'I see a man stepping forward with doves in his hands, which is a symbol that he is at peace and with God. He is smiling at you. He says you have a picture of him with you or you are carrying something of his.' This had to be right. In his experience of young widows they always seemed to carry a memento of their deceased loved one.

'You knew he loved you but he wasn't in your life as much as you wanted him to be. He wants you to know his life was complete when he left the physical world, and that he is supporting you in everything you do. You will never be able to break that bond. His soul will always be with you. Take what he gave you and allow it to start to heal,' he said, easing slightly forward in his seat for emphasis, his voice low and reassuring.

Turner had hit the emotional jackpot. She was hanging onto every word, her fingers now still, hands clasped together in her lap. Now adding a variety of loving messages and complimentary things from her late husband should give him a very successful reading. He would have to make it all up on the spot of course, but he was an expert at that. With no other clues to go on he took a chance.

'I feel something strange around here.' He used his hand to circle an area all around his chest and stomach to make the location as non-specific as possible. 'It's something I can't explain but it's like there is something not right there, something bad.' This ploy usually paid off – he'd found most early deaths had something to do with the heart, lungs, back or stomach and his motion was covering them all. Occasionally he'd get one with a head or neck trauma that he explained away as him sensing they were struggling to breathe. Either way he knew he couldn't lose.

Turner shrieked. He felt a stabbing pain in his abdomen and right shoulder. Involuntarily he rocked forward, gasping for breath, cradling his stomach with one hand and shoulder with the other. Then it was gone. This wasn't part of the act and he looked around quickly to see if anything externally had hit him. Nothing.

'I'm so sorry – I don't know what happened,' he spluttered, reaching under the table for a bottle of water. He sipped down the lukewarm liquid, trying to regain his composure. Feeling embarrassed he glanced sheepishly over at the girl.

She met his eyes with compassion. 'He had liver cancer. How could you know? Towards the end he had terrible pain in his stomach and shoulder. It was awful …' She was weeping openly now, living in the horror of her memories.

Desperately trying to regain control after his unexpected outburst his brain kicked into autopilot, and he began to reel out his practised stock phrases of comfort for the bereaved: 'He says you gave him that unconditional love that provided him with the strength to be who he was in the physical world. He wants me to thank you for remembering him every day. Actually, he's just leant over and kissed you and said he's sorry for leaving you.' This was working and he could see her physically relax into the chair as he was still wincing from the pain in his gut.

With no more information to go on and worried he'd have another painful spasm, he needed to end this fast and clean. 'I know you have other places to be so perhaps we had better leave it there. I am very sorry for your loss and I wish you the best.'

'I'm so grateful to you. You don't know what this means. It's so nice to know he's always around me, looking after me. Nice to know I'm not alone. Thanks so much.' Now the hard bitter exterior of their initial meeting was replaced with warmth and gratitude. She pushed over four hundred dollars.

'Please, this is too much. I'm only glad to use my gift to help you.' In truth he was much happier about the money.

'No, take it. I feel like a weight has been lifted from me.' And with that she was off without a backward glance.

Turner felt exhausted and more than a little worried that he had some kind of tummy bug from his foraging at the hotel buffet the previous evening. All this mental gymnastics and educated guesswork wore him out. Swiftly packing up his Gladstone briefcase he headed for the nearest bar, gingerly feeling his abdomen for any signs of soreness.

The casino was now alive with a sea of people whooping and hollering at the craps table and chatting enthusiastically to the smartly dressed dealers at the blackjack tables. Sitting heavily on an empty stool at the sports bar he ordered a double Crown Royal Whisky neat, then settled back to watch the baseball game on the large plasma TV behind the bar. Just as he got comfortable, someone knocked his elbow, spilling a little of his drink onto the video poker machine built into the counter of the bar.

He turned to see a stunning blonde in a tartan mini skirt gazing back at him, all innocence personified. 'I'm so sorry,' she said huskily, lustfully looking him up and down. 'My names Amy. What's yours?'

Turner's only answer was to down his drink in one and head off sullenly to his room alone, muttering 'bloody Vegas' under his breath.

CHAPTER 2

THE STEWARDESS

Turner woke sharply at dawn the next day as the sun streamed through the tinted hotel windows, flooding his huge room with the warm glow of the early morning light. He never bothered to close the curtains, either when he travelled or at home, preferring to live by the rhythmic patterns of light and dark that nature provided. With two shuffles and a little leap, he made it across the king-size bed to the safety of the floor before trotting to the bathroom. An hour and a half later, he was showered, shaved, dressed, packed and on his way down to the lobby to check out. It was his last day and, with an afternoon flight home, this morning would be his only free vacation time of the five-day trip.

He was an expert at packing, always managing to fit everything he needed into a shabby olive shoulder bag. After two disastrous trips, where his suitcases had disappeared into the airlines' missing-luggage black hole, he refused to ever check a bag again. The canvas bag was just large enough to squeeze in his Gladstone briefcase, toiletries and a few clothes, everything he needed for a few days away. It had handled storms, snow and baking heat and was still small enough to take as airline carry-on.

With the tattered luggage slung carelessly over his shoulder, he grabbed one of the waiting cabs and headed for Skips on Desert Avenue. From its birth around 1850 in Reno,

Nevada, making saddles and western boots, Skips had moved with the times, got rid of the saddle business and become the world's premier western boot and clothing store. Turner adored it – to him it was as good as having your own personalised fashion boutique.

His cab pulled into the huge parking lot outside the enormous façade of the famous store. Four grandiose brick archways surrounded an even bigger central one that had 'Skips' written plainly in huge red arcing capital letters on white facing. 'Western wear' was spelled out below with one word straddling each side of the main entrance. A terracotta pot with a healthy-looking green cactus decorated the foot of each monumental arch, the spiny plants thriving in the desert heat. The store didn't actually open until 10 am but Bill Coates, who managed the store, had become a good friend and drinking partner a few years back, after Turner had helped Bill's wife connect with her recently deceased father.

He had the store to himself and a twenty per cent discount courtesy of the manager. Suspended fluorescent lighting lit the interior as bright as daylight and pale wood partitions contrasted beautifully with the mixture of denim clothing and sparkling jewellery displays. Feeling excited, like a child does just before Christmas, he quickly made his way to the cowboy boot section at the far end of the store. Wood panelling similar to a weathered barn filled this feature wall topped with a burnt-in version of the Skips logo of a bull's head facing forward in brown silhouette. At various points large sets of nails had been hammered in and each pair supported one style of top-brand cowboy boots. Bill came scooting around the corner from behind a pile of white boxes. 'This what you'se looking for, partner?' he said in a mock Texas drawl and a huge infectious grin on his face (he was actually from Chicago). In his large hands he held two exquisite boots the like Turner had not seen before. They were calf length, the upper part made of a soft goat leather stained brown and then embossed with a stunning flaming design. The broad rounded toes were covered in shaded rattlesnake skin and the diamond pattern was so well done it looked rather like a fine Roman mosaic. 'Sold,' he beamed and put them on.

Turner handed him his old pair and Bill promptly threw them in the trash. The best way Turner knew to get exotic skin products through customs was to wear them! After adding a couple of pairs of boot-cut denim jeans to his haul, Bill waved him off to the airport.

McCarran International Airport at the south end of Vegas looks exactly like what it is – a pile of air-conditioned boxes in the middle of a desert, designed to pass people through with minimum fuss. The shining example of modern efficiency was the new Terminal 3 building used to handle all international passengers. It was organised and clean, with throngs of people from all over the world moving rapidly through at all hours of day and night. Turner headed past the sliding doors and welcomed the cool breeze of the air conditioning after a clammy walk from the taxi rank outside. He quickly scanned the departure board, looking for Virgin Atlantic Flight VS044.

After whisking through check-in he was off to face the scourge of the frequent traveller, the X-ray scanners. The guard at his station looked tired and disinterested, with a waistline that was so huge it probably had its own gravitational pull.

How the hell he would chase any would-be troublemaker was beyond him. Throwing his battered olive bag onto the conveyor that fed the security machine, Turner and his rattlesnake-skin boots walked unmolested into the boarding area.

His best friend and crazy guitarist Lee Melone had given him a duty-free shopping list that summed up his passions outside of music – whisky and cigars. Turner had never smoked so Lee had given him specific instructions on what to buy. Looking across the myriad of colourful boxes, he finally found a brand that met the description. Each cigar was cosily cocooned in an aluminium tube to keep the tobacco fresh. These suited Lee down to the ground as when he'd been gigging regularly he'd stash a couple in his shirt pocket for before and after gigs and they'd keep in perfect condition despite the clammy conditions of the venue. Finally, with his duty-free stash and olive bag in hand, he boarded the plane and headed straight up the stairs of the Boeing 747, looking for premium economy and his seat at the rear of the cabin, next to the window.

Half the seats were already occupied with various suited business types scattered amongst the hungover tourists. As usual, no one was talking. Turner had witnessed the same phenomenon in doctors' waiting rooms and public transport back in England. Put a crowd of strangers together and the one thing you could almost guarantee is that they wouldn't talk to each other. He eased into his chair after wedging his bags carefully into the overhead compartment. Within about five minutes he had been joined by his flight companion, a tanned sixty-something lady of medium build, dressed in a smart blue business suit with a colourful Versace silk scarf around her neck. She nodded politely at him and smiled, as travelling neighbours meeting on a plane for the first time are wont to do. As with all the other passengers, the pleasantries stopped there as both of them sized each other up as potential nut cases who might jabber on incessantly throughout the long flight. Turner's Hawaiian shirt and cowboy boots seemed to have quite an alarming effect on her, and thankfully she just sat down quietly and didn't attempt to engage him in any more conversation. It was just before midnight back home and he adjusted his watch to UK time to try and get his body clock back in sync. After gratefully accepting the orange juice offered by a blonde-haired stewardess, he built a snuggly nest out of the pillow and blanket the airline had supplied and settled down to sleep.

Six hours later, the entire cabin began to shake like a child's toy as the plane hit major turbulence over the Atlantic. The fasten-seatbelt light blinked urgently into action and two of the overhead lockers sprung open, spewing their contents onto the corridor floor. The rush of air outside buffeted the huge wings, rattling and roaring against the thin metal as it went. Ice was gradually forming and creeping up the window, and streaks of hail hammered the outside of the pane.

Turner looked around quickly at his seated companion, who was desperately clutching a set of rosewood rosary beads, mumbling prayers under her breath. Instinctively, he reached out and grabbed her hand and smiled. She jolted from the surprising human contact and then grabbed his hand as if her very survival depended on it. Turner could see that at one time she had been a truly beautiful woman. Now the ravages of time had wrinkled her complexion, making her look much older than she was – the crow's feet around her eyes were more like raven's feet with hobnail boots on. He guessed the scarf was there to cover a similar effect on her neck. Faint crease lines around her upper lip suggested she was either a smoker or ex-smoker. The only smell he could sense was a waft of her delicate Dior perfume, so he suspected the latter. They sat like this, holding hands and nodding and smiling, as hell broke loose outside the aircraft.

'*Merci, monsieur. J'étais tellement peur,*' she mumbled in a soft trembling voice. Turner shook his head and gave a gentle shrug of his shoulders to signal he did not understand. Reaching into her handbag, she took out a brown moleskin pocketbook and a small blue pen. With deft strokes, she wrote 'Sophia' then pointed from the notebook to herself. He nodded, picked up the pen and wrote 'Nathen Turner'. She smiled and laughed at their little childhood game of 'guess-a-sketch' and said 'Nathen,' reaching out to shake hands as if formally introducing herself. Her palm felt dry and soft against his, and she had stopped shaking. Outside the weather was easing and the plane resumed its smooth motion across the skies.

Quickly she sketched an outline of the Eiffel Tower, pointed to herself, made a flapping motion with her arms and laughed again. So she was flying to Paris via London, he guessed. Turner drew a large question mark and spelt out Las Vegas in capitals to ask why she had visited the American playground. Quickly she outlined a remarkably accurate replica of a roulette table including the wheel, spinning ball and number table with chips laid on it. Reaching into her bag again she pulled out a gold-card membership from the Monte Carlo casino on the main strip. He knew these were as rare as hen's teeth and only reserved for the big players. Holders of the card were granted the best luxury suites, free room service and complimentary bar as well as invitations to a series of private gambling parties. His mouth attempted silently to say 'Oh' and 'Wow' at the same time but ultimately he just looked like a goldfish swallowing a large apple.

At this precise time a stewardess appeared on her regular drink run up and down the cabin. Turner looked up just in time to see her burst into hysterical laughter at the goldfish expression on his face and the little book of drawings held gingerly by Sophia. The stewardess just couldn't help herself and was holding her stomach and lolling from side to side. Turner thought she was the most attractive and sexiest woman he had ever seen, even though she seemed to find him an object of extreme hilarity. Long ebony hair, immaculately groomed and tied back in a tight bun, framed her beautiful oval face and high cheekbones that gave away her Japanese origins. The most striking thing was the colour of her eyes. They were a beautiful shade of deep green, the type of eyes a man could lose his soul too. He had never seen a green-eyed Asian person before and wondered briefly what bizarre genetic mutation had caused that way back in her ancestry. Whatever or whoever it was, he was extremely grateful. She was absolutely stunning.

Emiko Akiyama daintily straightened the creases in her red stewardess uniform but did not notice that the top button of her double-breasted jacket had come undone from her jocular fit, exposing a tantalising glimpse of her breast and a black lacy bra. Turner had most definitely noticed and his eyes had opened even wider, spawning another fit of hysterics from the stewardess. Her gold name badge jiggled up and down and his gaze followed the movement with intense concentration. It simply said 'Emiko Akiyama', with 'Jade' written centrally underneath – he assumed correctly that the latter was a nickname based on the unique colour of her eyes.

'I'm so sorry,' she said in perfect English with a slight American twang, 'but you looked really funny sitting there with that expression on your face. Are you playing a game?' She looked at the notebook with its scribbled images. Turner attempted to regain his composure but it wasn't easy now she was even closer to him. She smelt of roses and lavender and her smooth soft skin was taking his mind to more testosterone-fuelled thoughts. Sophia began to talk in French and to his total surprise Jade answered fluently. They chattered quickly, giggling to themselves. All he could make out was the odd phrase like *'bel homme'* and *'très drôle'* as she gestured at him.

'How wonderful! Thank you sir. The lady says you have been a huge comfort to her.' Jade seemed positively delighted at his fumbling attempts to communicate with his fellow passenger.

'I'm Nathen, Nathen Turner. I don't speak French … we were just trying to find a way to talk to each other …' he stammered, catching his breath and going slightly pink in the cheek. Beaming warmly at him she reached out to shake his hand. It felt so soft in his that he held it longer than perhaps he ought to have.

'I'm Jade – we'll be landing in about an hour. Can I get you anything to drink?' she said, regaining her composure and now back in professional stewardess mode. Turner ordered a green tea, which seemed to meet with her approval, and became absorbed by the rhythmic swinging motion of her red skirt as she walked back to the galley.

For the rest of the flight he occupied himself with watching Jade as best he could without looking too much like a crazed stalker. She already thought he was a joke and he didn't want her to think he was a pervert as well. The plane finally descended, making his ears pop, and bounced noisily onto the runway at Gatwick. Waiting patiently until the fasten-seatbelt sign went off, he watched Sophia grab her luggage before retrieving his own from the overhead locker. As he swung his long legs out into the aisle the heel of his boot caught on a small orange brocade handkerchief that had fallen to the floor under his travelling companion's seat. Scanning across the quickly exiting passengers he could see no sign of Sophia. Thinking he would easily catch up with her at passport control he quickly pushed the colourful handkerchief into his jeans pocket.

Jade was standing at the top of the stairs, thanking everyone for flying with Virgin as they disembarked. As he walked up to say his farewells, she leant forward and gently pushed a folded yellow sheet of paper in his hand. Her breath was on his neck as she whispered, 'Look, I feel really bad – I'm sorry I laughed at you. You seem like a really nice guy the way you helped that French lady. Give me a call if you are in town anytime and maybe we can go out for a drink or something to make up for it. It could be fun to get to know you better. My phone number is on the paper.'

Nothing like this had ever happened to him before, but he tried to act cool, as if beautiful women were always giving him their phone numbers. She didn't really know anything about him and just seemed to have accepted him as a nice, fun guy without him resorting to sleazy psychic manipulation techniques to grab her attention. Turner felt clean and invigorated; it was so refreshing for him not to have to lie and put on an act.

'I'd love to,' he said enthusiastically, 'but you're buying the first round. Us northern boys can't afford London prices!' She laughed again, kissed him on the cheek and squeezed his hand in farewell.

There was no sign of his French companion outside the plane. In his romantic trance, he'd completely forgotten she was en route to Paris and would be halfway across the airport by now, looking for her connecting flight. Feeling a little guilty for not being able to return the handkerchief, he made his way to the car park then climbed into his silver VW Golf and headed out on to the M25 motorway. As the lights turned red he only had one colour on his mind, and that was green – in particular a beautiful, sexy Jade green.

CHAPTER 3

THE MUSICIAN

As Turner's plane was hitting the tarmac in London, two hundred and fifty miles north in the beautiful coastal town of Whitby, a different scene was unfolding for his best friend Lee Melone. The raucous squawking of sea gulls was slowly waking him from a deep alcohol-fuelled sleep. 'Kitti-wake, kitti-wake', the high-pitched screeching said over and over again.

Slowly, he opened one eye and cautiously looked around. He was in his own room, which was always a good sign, but he was naked and ice cold, goose pumps prickling his flesh. Gradually, he levered open the other eyelid and immediately wished he hadn't. His black electric guitar appeared to be doing obscene things to the rear end of his girlfriend's teddy bear and what looked like his underwear had been used as a makeshift blindfold around its furry little head.

'What the hell!' he mumbled with a mouth as dry as sandpaper. The sound of his voice was like a gunshot going off in his brain. He couldn't feel his arm and was starting to panic before realising he was lying on it. The putrid stench of stale cigar smoke filled the room, and an empty bottle of whisky was strewn carelessly on the floor at the foot of the bed. Sliding out of bed with a bump onto the ground, he crawled to the windowsill, his bare behind shining whitely in the daylight that was streaming through gaps in the curtains. From a flower vase on the windowsill he grabbed a plastic rose and began to shake it violently. After about a minute, the end of a thin white marijuana joint poked out the bottom of the deliberately hollowed stem. More frantic shaking and it fell to the floor. Gratefully, he picked it up and continued his snake-like crawl to the bedside table, desperately hunting for his lighter. It had been stuck upright in a half-eaten bowl of peanuts and he reached over and flicked the flame. The sudden brightness made him wince as he lit the skinny spliff and inhaled deeply. Acrid smoke hit the back of his dry throat, making him cough and splutter, but he kept inhaling. The effects of the drug jangled through his nerves, kicking his blunted senses back into action. Slumping back down with his back against the bedside table he tilted his head, slowly exhaling the thick grey smoke up towards the ceiling.

The bedroom door crashed open and a huge dog bounded enthusiastically into the room and ran straight at him. Light flooded the room from the open door and silhouetted the hellhound that had broken his morning reverie. Continuing its straight-ahead route, the dog's huge furry front paw stepped between his open naked legs, causing him to squeal in pain as he turned just in time to avoid the wet slippery tongue kissing him square on the lips. It was licking his face as if its very life depended on it and the sopping drool began to drip thickly onto his bare chest. The worst thing was the smell – its breath was a mixture of the inside of a stale sardine can and sweaty feet.

'For God's sake, Kyle, get off me,' he said, pushing hard to his feet, his head spinning, trying desperately to regain some sort of authority. It worked for the bloody dog whisperer he'd seen on TV but his hairy companion just ignored him and wagged its tail. Standing there naked, his large manhood swinging just in front of the dog's face and a smoking spliff in his hand was when things really took a turn for the worst.

'Explain!' One simple word like a lightning bolt came from the direction of the open door. Sandra Vaughan stood hands on hips, legs astride, her eyes blazing daggers at the chaotic scene. Instinctively, he shot both hands over his naked genitals, forgetting he had the lighted joint in one of them. Another squeal of pain followed by choice swearing didn't seem to be helping his case but the dog was loving this game, its tail accelerating to full windscreen-wiper speed. Sandra's full breasts were thrust indignantly upward; she wore a thin shirt that stopped just above her hips, exposing a sexy triangle of skimpy pink knickers underneath. His manhood was starting to react to this vision of seething sex goddess, so he pushed his cupped hands harder over his crotch, having now quickly stuck the smoking spliff in his mouth. The smoke was making his eyes water, but he didn't dare reach for it in case it exposed the evidence of his swelling loins. Truth was, he had no idea how he'd got home, why he was naked and why the teddy bear would be in therapy for the rest of its cute furry little life. He simply bowed his head, muttering sheepishly, 'I'm sorry.'

She exploded into laughter. Sandra had seen him like this many, many times in their two-year relationship. At only five feet three inches she was a mini powerhouse of blonde, blue-eyed Australian sexiness and when she turned it on she knew she could wrap Lee around her small and expertly manicured finger. They had first met about three years ago when she was doing bar work at the Jolly Roger pub on Whitby's West Cliff and his band the Hep Cats were playing the evening gig. She'd only been in the country a few months and had worked her way north, taking any cleaning or bar jobs that would feed her and keep a roof over her head. Her plan was to work in the UK for a year then head home to Cairns and work on the tourist diving boats serving the Barrier Reef while she was still under thirty and fit enough to do it. Their first meeting didn't go well as he was angry as hell about the gig. His band were really called the Hip Cats, in a throwback to the swinging sixties and an expression Jimi Hendrix used to use. Some dyslexic kid at the poster printing office had spelt it 'Hep' instead of 'Hip' so Hep Cats they were. He hated it, but it stuck.

They met again when his band swung back into town and had a steamy alcohol-fuelled one-night stand. Although it was lust at first pint that night, their relationship grew and two months later they moved in together in a terraced house on Whitby's East Cliff, up towards the ruined abbey made famous by Bram Stoker's *Dracula* novel. Sandra could walk to her bar work across the small swing bridge that connected the two sides of the town, and he was enjoying putting down roots for the first time. Everything was fine until about a year ago. Tony, his long-time drummer and school friend, decided that doing massive quantities of LSD washed down with rum would make him an expert driver. Tony had struggled with drug issues for years, sucked in first by the rock and roll myth that substance abuse made you cool. High on his chemical cocktail he'd driven his car straight off the beach cliffs at Flamborough Head, probably trying to avoid the imaginary dragons and monkeys that were chasing it down the road. Lee had to identify the body, and swore he would never do hard drugs again. This hadn't quite worked out as he still lapsed into smoking the odd joint here and there, but that remained his limit.

Lee didn't have the stomach to go on with the band without Tony; it would just never be the same. So he was basically out of work with no savings and no prospects. Whilst drowning his sorrows over a bottle of whisky with his only other surviving long-term school friend, Nathen Turner, the two had hatched a plan that would work for both of them. At the time, Turner was holed up in a small one-bed apartment down the coast at Filey. Just him and his large dog, Kyle, in a small one-bedroom flat was not a great combination. Turner had rescued Kyle from a Dogs Trust centre a couple of years ago when he'd felt lonely and couldn't find the right woman to share his life with. He'd decided a dog was the next best thing for now and took pity on the half Siberian Husky, half Rottweiler mongrel puppy whom everybody else seemed terrified of. So they had figured that if Turner and his dog moved in with Lee and Sandra it would solve their immediate financial crisis, and they could look after the dog when he was travelling. The terraced house was in a great location overlooking the bay and had more than enough room with four floors and a small garden at the back. Also Lee could help manage Turner's psychic fair work and private party gigs as he had loads of experience looking after the band's touring schedule and great contacts in the entertainment business. Lee knew that the readings and psychic mumbo jumbo Turner did were simply a show he put on; so how could it be much different from arranging gigs for the band? Lee agreed to take a twenty per cent cut of the profits, and that would more than keep him financially secure. The only issue they'd had was that Turner hated drug use so Lee had to find increasingly weird and wonderful hiding places for his stash of pot. So far, his fake flower ruse had remained undiscovered and a large supply of air fresheners had helped mask the accusing scent.

'Nathen's rang,' Sandra said simply, thrusting her breasts even higher in the air. 'He's on the way north now – should be here by about five o'clock, he reckons. He asked if we want to try that new Chinese restaurant in Scarborough tonight – his treat. Apparently, Vegas went well and he's got a pocketful of cash burning a hole in his trousers.'

Lee looked at her, relieved now that she seemed back to her normal self and wasn't going to roast his ass for whatever he'd done (which he still had no memory of). As he didn't have the courage to speak to her, he just silently nodded his head in agreement.

'Now we've got that sorted perhaps you'd like to demonstrate what you were doing to Mr Teddy last night.' As Lee had begun to relax his hands had dropped to his sides unconsciously and his large manhood was now at full mast in response to her sexy outfit. Sandra brushed Kyle out the door, deftly flicking it closed with her foot as she stalked sexily towards him. He could smell her natural musk as she pounced, her soft breasts pushing against his naked chest.

'Come on,' she said, her voice a silky tease, 'We've only got about two hours before he gets here …' pushing him back down onto the bed, straddling his legs.

Lee imagined he could hear the gulls outside change their squawking to 'Cor, Cor' as she wriggled and moaned over his prone naked body. Lying back contentedly, he silently thanked whichever god had brought this Australian vixen into his life.

CHAPTER 4

THE CHINA ROSE

'She did what?' Lee exploded, spitting half his spicy prawn ball across the table in shock.

'She gave me her number and asked me to call her next time I'm in London – honestly, for real …' even as Turner said the words, he couldn't believe it himself. He hadn't been able to stop thinking about Jade since leaving the airport.

'So a gorgeous Asian chick takes a liking to you and you haven't even pulled any of your usual psychic crap on her?' Lee was referring to the way Turner normally tried to tempt women into his life using his cold reading techniques to establish a rapport quickly. This would normally lead on to him offering to read their palm, which they very rarely refused, and this skin to skin contact would often develop into contact of a more carnal nature. The only problem was that the relationships never lasted once the sex dried up, as it always did after a couple of months. They'd demand he read their future or tell them what their aura was like today before bringing in their friends and relatives and asking him to do it for them as well. It just ground Turner down – he always had to end it, unable to sustain the lie without the physical side to distract him.

'She doesn't even know what I do …' he continued, explaining again for the third time to Lee exactly what had happened. Sandra Vaughan watched the pair of them in

34

silent amusement. They were always like this when they got together. She looked at them sitting in similar floral blue Tommy Bahama Hawaiian shirts, leaning excitedly across the table and chattering away like two school children discussing the latest cool trend.

Turner had arrived at the house late afternoon and thrown his bags into the kitchen before being flattened and licked half to death by the dog. After a quick shower and change of clothing they were heading to the restaurant. It was Thursday so the weekend crowds wouldn't arrive until tomorrow and that suited the trio just fine. The east coast became a thriving mass of day-trippers and caravans Friday through Sunday during the holiday season, and every form of human life seemed to congregate in the towns. It would not be unusual to see goths, hen parties, pensioners and families with young excited children all sitting playing Bingo, or some other godforsaken seaside game, at one of the crowded amusement arcades that lined the sea fronts. Thankfully, it just looked like the usual mixed bag of locals in tonight so Turner, Lee, and Sandra could have their choice of table.

The restaurant itself had originally been a petrol station on the Whitby-to-Scarborough coast road before it had fallen into financial trouble and was bought out by a Chinese family in the new year. For the last six months, a team of builders, electricians and interior decorators had been hard at work to bring The China Rose to life, proudly offering 'Authentic Asian Cuisine' on the purple neon sign that sat above the main entrance. The inside was beautiful, with red and black lacquer wood panels supporting pagoda-shaped archways that led from one dining area to another. On a raised platform at the rear of the main room, a gigantic marine fish tank had been installed, running the entire length of one wall. It truly was a spectacle and a remarkable piece of engineering and design. A long stretch of coral reef sat on virgin pale sand inhabited by hunched hermit crabs and darting striped prawns with their feelers constantly tapping out for food. Colourful fish swam in and out of the waving anemones, playing in the stream of air bubbles coming from the under reef aerators, the whole tank bursting with salty life. Two or three circular black lacquer dining tables had been placed close by, and it was at one of these the friends sat in the blue glow that cascaded from the tank's lights.

'So you haven't called her yet? Are you crazy?' Lee was still in shock but had pulled himself together enough to stuff another spicy pork ball into his mouth and munch aggressively.

'It's not like that – she's different. She doesn't know anything about the psychic stuff I do. Once she does I'm not sure she will want any part of it. Plus I live two hundred and fifty miles away at a seaside resort best known for a black jewellery stone and a blood-sucking immortal – not exactly the heady heights of London's night life!' He was referring to the black jet that had put Whitby's jewellery business on the map and Dracula. As he mentioned the latter, he made a comic biting gesture as if he had fangs on his front teeth. Sandra cracked up laughing.

'You mean to tell me that Mr Tinkie's been on bread and water for six long months since you split from that loony hippy Zoe at Christmas, and you still haven't bloody called her? Man, if you don't get a woman soon you're going to explode.' To emphasise his disbelief Lee mimed an exploding gesture from the general direction of his loins.

Sandra started to snort and gag with laughter as Lee's hands were gesturing upwards and he mouthed the word 'boom'. A very smart older lady in a casual white patterned blouse and below-the-knee navy-blue pencil skirt approached the table hesitantly. Turner turned around, sensing the presence just in time to see the look of horror cross her face at Lee's wild gesticulations. Turner recognised her immediately and blushed slightly.

'Mrs Armstrong, I'm so sorry. He doesn't get out much, and we have to keep him caged in the basement most days.' They all laughed again, breaking the tension and easing his embarrassment.

Juliet Armstrong ran the Oswin Hall Hotel in the heart of Whitby with her husband Bill. The original Oswin Tudor manor house dated back to around 1650 and the beamed ceilings and stone-mullioned windows had proved a popular draw for Turner's ghost-hunting talks. The atmosphere and layout of the hotel and its traditional furnishings provided a near perfect setting for groups of amateur ghost hunters expertly led by Turner through the dark corridors and echoing rooms. While exploring with his range of pseudo-scientific devices borrowed from The Alchemist, the spiritual shop in Grape Lane, he would whisper tales of the headless ghost of traitor Bill McBride, one of the previous seventeenth-century owners that reputedly roamed the corridors at night. As the groups imagined feeling this frightening presence drifting silently through the building, Turner would build the tension even more by adding in other folk tales that surrounded Oswin

Hall's history – mysterious footsteps, the sounds of children playing in empty rooms and various recorded sightings of poltergeist activity. It was great business for Turner, and he could be doing three or four of these a week in the height of the tourist season. Juliet looked drawn and tired and was certainly the last person he would want to upset. It could cost him a small fortune in lost trade as the ghost hunts gave him free advertising to push his psychic parties as well. Turner began to sense something. A feeling of overwhelming grief surrounding his long-time business friend.

'You OK, Mrs Armstrong?' he asked gently, not wanting to point out her downtrodden bearing.

She leaned forward to make herself heard above the strains of the gentle Chinese melodies that drifted in the background. 'Did you sense anything about Bill?'

The strange phrasing of the question made him think. He hadn't been back long enough to catch up on the local gossip; obviously something had happened to her husband if she was asking him if he'd sensed anything. The likelihood was, it was unexpected and final. That coupled with her pale face and despairing manner made him certain he was right. Back into his psychic role, he answered quietly, 'He has passed into the spirit world, hasn't he? I'm so sorry. I can feel his loving presence still around you.'

She squeezed his hand. 'Thank you. I was sure you'd feel his spirit. It's been such a shock. When I saw you sitting here I just knew he'd have contacted you after all the years you've been friends. I found him dead in the flat on Monday.'

Turner just nodded back reassuringly as if he already had some inside spiritual knowledge of her husband's passing.

Inside himself, he was desperately trying to figure out what he should say next. He knew the flat she was talking about was a three-bedroom maisonette the Armstrongs had moved into when the two children had left home. They had previously stayed in Oswin Hall itself but soon realised that living and working in the same place without kids to distract them was not a great combination. The flats had formed part of an eighteenth-century townhouse conversion near the hotel, and they had taken the one on the top floor overlooking a walled garden and Pannett Park beyond. It was a beautiful setting and remarkably quiet considering how close it was to the town centre. Turner figured it was best if she did all the talking, so he got her a seat and asked her gently to explain all that had happened.

She went on to tell him how her husband had been complaining of a headache on the Monday morning and so she'd sent him home for painkillers and a lie-down in the flat with a request to come back and relieve her on reception at lunchtime. Twelve o'clock passed, and then one, and she had become worried, as he was always an excellent timekeeper. After trying to telephone the flat and getting no answer, she had grabbed one of the bar staff to cover reception and hurried the short distance across the road and down the narrow stone-walled path before climbing the two flights of stairs to their maisonette. The apartment entrance opened onto a small hall with the door to the lounge off to the right at the end facing the garden and park. She found him there, slumped in his usual dark red leather armchair, deathly cold and pallid. An empty water glass and the morning's paper were scattered carelessly at his feet and the right side of his face drooped grotesquely, dried drool staining the lower corner of his lips. She painted this horrific, graphic picture to Turner as if still reliving it in her mind, and the shock and pain were evident on her face. Saying it out loud seemed to be helping her slightly and she eased more upright to continue. A doctor had been called and the body moved to the local hospital. As with all sudden deaths, a post mortem was conducted and she'd only got the results that morning. The cause of death was a massive stroke, and they reassured her it would have been over very quickly and he would have felt no pain. Her friends had suggested they get her out for a while to try to lift her spirits, and they had ended up in The China Rose. At this, Turner turned around to his left and spotted the group of ladies anxiously watching her from one of the tables near the front of the restaurant. He gave them a little wave as if to say everything was all right then bent forward as she continued.

'The thing is, I don't feel like I've had a chance to say goodbye. He was here talking to me just as plain as you; then he was gone.' She started to sob again, her voice quavering. 'Please help me. I need to make contact with him on the other side and say my goodbyes – I feel so empty and alone. You're the only one I know who can help me – do you think you will be able to reach him for me in the spirit world?'

'Of course, Mrs Armstrong. I'd be delighted to help you make contact.' He smiled confidently at her. 'Please don't worry. Enjoy your meal tonight and Lee will call on you to make arrangements in the morning. Take care.' With that she left the diners happily like a huge weight had been lifted from her shoulders. Turner smiled to himself at his good fortune. He knew he didn't have any paying clients until the end of the following week so performing a séance to contact her dead husband would be an unexpected boost to his finances.

Sandra had a tear in her eye. 'Nathen that was so lovely. How did you know he was dead? Did you hear it on the car radio or something?'

Spotting an opportunity to get back to the gaiety of their previous conversation, Lee chimed in. 'Of course not! He's psychic, you know that right? He feels things,' and he winked secretly at Turner to play along. 'Sandra's had a psychic experience while you've been away, haven't you? Go on tell him …' Lee nudged her in encouragement.

'Well it's probably nothing really. I was sitting in the house waiting for Lee to get in and just started thinking of my mother back in Oz and what she'd be up to. Then the phone rang, and it was her! Just weird I guess.' She looked a little embarrassed.

Lee's eyes were boring into Turner's, trying to signal him to string her along. Turner got the message. 'Maybe you do have something. Everybody is capable of being a psychic; they just don't know how to develop their skills. Look, let's test you …' He pulled out the red notebook and pen from his rear jeans pocket and started to draw using elaborate movements of his hand. He kept the book close to his chest, with the solid back facing her so there was no way she could see what he was doing. 'I'm going to draw something and then send it to you psychically. If you can pick up an impression of what I've drawn, then you've definitely got some powers.' The pen moved up and down in random motions, stopping occasionally and then turning back to where it started.

Lee loved this. Watching Turner perform was like seeing a different person, not the easy-going guy with the offbeat fashion sense he knew and loved. Sandra was enthralled, totally bought in to the test she'd been asked to do.

'OK, I'm done.' He flattened the open book face down on the table in front of him. 'Close your eyes and take some deep breaths. Try not to think of anything. Let the image come to you.' Lee was miming a spooky 'woo' gesture with outstretched arms and wiggling fingers, taking advantage of the fact that Sandra couldn't see him.

She wrinkled her forehead in intense concentration, breathing deeply, eyes tight shut. Slowly she opened her eyes and looked back at the pair of serious faces studying her from across the table.

Turner opened his palms, forming a yoga-like pose. 'Now Sandra, concentrate. Can you tell me what I've drawn on the paper?'

She had to be honest; she hadn't felt anything. The only thoughts that had flashed into her head were about whether she'd have a dessert or not. Shrugging her shoulders, she simply said, 'No.'

Turner deftly flicked over the book to show he'd written the word 'NO' in huge capitals covering the entire page. 'My God, that's amazing. How the hell did you know that?'

The three of them erupted with laughter, the gloom of Mrs Armstrong's conversation evaporating into the night. Talk turned to catching up with other titbits of news and tall tails of Lee's antics and misbehaviour. Finally, armed with the remainder of the spicy pork balls wrapped up in silver foil for Kyle, they headed back to the car to find him fast asleep with his head resting gently between his paws on the back seat.

CHAPTER 5

SUMMONING THE SPIRITS

The following morning, Lee in his role as Turner's 'Psychic Booking Agent' called in on Juliet Armstrong to find her alone, nursing a cup of tea in the kitchen of her flat. For things as personal as this he never used the coldness of a telephone call, much preferring the human touch. His job was to gather as much information as he could for Turner and agree the fee in as sympathetic a way as possible. Keeping Turner away from the client until the actual 'performance' always worked well. By the time Turner arrived, they'd always forgotten anything they'd told Lee. Turner could then replay the information as if he was being told it by whatever spirit he was pretending to conjure up. After Lee accepted her kind offer of a drink, they made their way solemnly to the lounge.

'He was here, Lee, in that chair,' she said, gesturing at a comfortable king-size Chesterfield armchair. She was trying desperately to hold back her grief and had obviously been busy tidying up as the entire room was spotless.

'Mrs Armstrong, do you have anything of Bill's that we could use to strengthen the spiritual connection during the séance? Something he handled every day that had some kind of meaning to him? Often we leave some of our energy in the things we care about, and we can use this to strengthen the spiritual bridge between the two worlds.' Lee was well versed in how to set the stage for psychic events. Using familiar

43

objects to channel the departed had proved a fantastic convincer in the minds of the bereaved.

'Probably this I think …' She moved to grab an object on top of the white marble fireplace. It was a glossy black intricately carved box of possibly Scandinavian origin. A Celtic knot design was expertly chiselled into the lid, covering it almost from corner to corner. More linking and swirling patterns decorated the four sides. In stark contrast to the rest of the box, the plain bottom was smooth and polished to a glossy black mirror finish. Even from where Lee sat he could see it looked old, ancient dust lining the deep recesses around the shapes. Opening it, she tipped out a set of car keys onto the chair and handed the box to him.

Lee accepted it as if receiving a precious and fragile sculpture. 'Why was this particularly important to your husband, Mrs Armstrong? We have to make sure we use the most appropriate item, so I apologise if the question upsets you.'

'He was fascinated by it. Watch …' She lifted it from Lee and gently rocked it from side to side. The box let out a quiet rattle in time with her movements. Flicking open the lid again to prove it was empty, she continued to tilt it, accompanied again by the noise. 'He could never understand why it rattled when it was empty. First he thought there was something trapped inside but the box is completely sealed – see …' She turned it over in her hands close to his face. There were no visible screws to take the wood apart, and the interior was expertly lined with red silk. It certainly was unusual, Lee thought.

'Where did he buy it?' he asked, thinking maybe this

could be a future source of unusual objects for Turner's work.

'That's just it. He didn't. We found it about twenty years ago, tucked away behind a headboard in one of our hotel rooms. A young Asian student had been staying for the goth festival, and the cleaner spotted it when she was making up the room for the next guest. The girl left without any goodbye – they all tended to do that back then. Typical teenagers heading for the next thing on their hectic social calendar; you know what it's like. We tried to return it, but in those days we weren't too hot on taking visitors' personal details as long as they paid up front for the room. Different times now though. I'm sure the hotel inspectors will have us fingerprinting people before long – health and safety rules have just gone crazy in the last few years. They'll have me risk-assessing pouring a pint of beer next.' She shook her head, lost in thought at the administration hoops she had to go through just to allow someone to stay in the hotel.

Lee smiled at her remark; her resentment for bureaucracy seemed to be overcoming her grief for a short while. 'You know, Lee, back then it was perfectly acceptable to have one sheet of paper with a name and room number in the hotel register. Now things are just crazy with stupid European Law requirements taking priority over whether the guests actually have a good time. Simpler times, eh?'

Lee nodded and after a brief discussion on how things were much better in the old days and agreeing the psychic's fee he left her smiling on the doorstep, promising that Turner would be over the next evening to do the séance.

Twenty-four hours later, Turner was dressed as sombre as he ever got with a black Hawaiian shirt decorated with aboriginal white-silhouetted patterns, black jeans, concho belt and his new rattlesnake skin boots. Underneath the shirt was a black T-shirt – actually a Hep Cats print fan shirt, but the logo was hidden by the buttoned outer garment – topped off with a hammered silver Ethiopian Coptic cross necklace he'd got from one of the hippy stalls on the market. His shoulder-length blonde hair was neatly combed with just a suitable amount of gelled disarray to make him look trendy.

He had walked in the cool night air across the river bridge from his house to get to the maisonette carrying his battered brown leather Gladstone briefcase containing his standard séance kit – candles, velvet drapes and a TriField meter. The meter was internally similar in design to the kind used by builders and ardent do-it-yourself types to find hidden electrical wiring or plumbing pipes. It scanned the spectrum looking for any disturbance in the electromagnetic field and when it did a shrill alarm sounded. What was peculiar about this one is it could scan both AC and DC fields. This characteristic had made it a prime tool for would-be ghost hunters. The theory, as he vaguely understood it, was that human senses only see a very tiny part of the energy fields that are around us. So for example, although we know things like ultra-violet radiation exist we can only sense it when it burns skin after too much sun exposure. Things like mobile phone, radio and TV transmissions envelope us, but again we cannot sense them without having a device tuned to do so. The meter worked the same way except it was tuned in to find energy fields from ghosts. This of course was pure conjecture, as nobody knew what energy the spirit world gave off. But it was a great way to sell the meters to gullible spiritual types and a perfect prop for people like Turner. He'd installed a simple electrical modification so he could set it off at will with a small hidden button on the base of the unit. Not surprisingly, Turner always found ghosts with the help of this covert modification.

Arriving at the flat, he'd found Juliet Armstrong also dressed in black. She looked pale in a tight wool suit with a lacy blouse underneath and wore no jewellery except her wedding ring. Talking to each other in hushed church-like whispers, she'd helped him black out the windows with the velvet drapes. Then he had used the meter to demonstrate how it could pick up electrical wiring before turning the black selector knob to the DC setting as he explained that this was the one they needed to spot spiritual energy. Scanning with the blue-faced meter in the palm of his hand, they both watched the needle as it registered nothing until he approached the leather armchair. As soon as he got close to it the meter gave out a high-pitched alarm, making Juliet jump, and the needle swung to the highest point of the scale. Turner had backed off from the chair, releasing the hidden switch as he did so, and the meter had dropped quickly back to zero. This was enough to convince Juliet that some spiritual essence of her husband remained centred on the chair he'd died in. Together they pulled it into the middle of the room, and she watched him silently go about the macabre ritual of placing a wide purple candle at each corner of the base.

'Mrs Armstrong, Lee mentioned you had an object of your husband's we could use to draw his spirit close to us. May I have it, please?' She handed the carved black box down from the fireplace. As Turner took it he could hear the strange rattle his friend had mentioned, and he couldn't help himself turning it upside down to look for the source of the noise. With no obvious explanation, he gently placed it on the seat of the Chesterfield armchair. To his embarrassment, years of use had created a backward slope on the seat cushion and the smooth bottom of the box slid quickly to the rear with a thud.

Wondering what to do, he rooted around in his briefcase and found the orange brocade handkerchief from the plane stuffed untidily in the bottom. He must have thrown it in when he unpacked and then forgotten all about it. Thankful for the discovery, he laid it centrally on the seat cushion and then placed the glossy box on top. The elaborately stitched pattern on the handkerchief created enough grip to stop the box sliding down again, and he sighed with relief.

As he lit the candles, Juliet flicked off the room light. The quivering candlelight flooded her face as she peered over the chair, shadows filling her eye sockets, giving her a strange skull-like expression. It was easy to imagine the flickering patterns in the corners of the room creating recognisable shapes, the same way children imagine weird monsters and strange faces in cloud formations. The oscillating shadows mingled into one another around the marble fire surround, and Turner believed he could see the shape of a huge beast emerging with a grotesque head and two large horns. Even he was not immune to the way our senses play tricks in the dark.

They stood together, heads bowed. Turner reached out gently for her hand and she gratefully accepted it with a little squeeze. Softly he began to speak, his rhythmic chanting filling the room.

'*Spiritus meus, Audi vocem meam, et mecum ad te. Ostende mihi si audiat*,' he almost sang over and over again. He had learned the rhythmic way of talking by listening to Gregorian monk CDs and the words were his own, which roughly translated meant, 'Spirits hear my prayer. Join me with you and listen to my voice. If you can hear me, please show me now.' An old schoolteacher friend had translated them into Latin – he always thought this was more effective for his clients as many of them were used to this type of phrasing and language in church.

For five minutes he kept this up, the words rhythmical, the timbre soft like talking to a lover. The silent room echoed no reply. Then slowly from the gloom a soft knocking could be heard – tap ... tap ... tap it went, like someone gently trying to knock on the door. Juliet shivered, and her hand tensed in his. The tapping continued slowly and gently, forcing them to concentrate. It was difficult trying to hear any sound clearly above the calls of the Saturday revellers filtering in from outside.

'Bill, can you hear me? I have Juliet with me and she wants to speak with you. Is that you making the tapping? If it is, please tap once only for yes.' Silence ... and then one single tap slightly louder than before. They waited to see if more followed it but only the oppressive quiet filled the room.

She was gripping his hand harder and harder and her shaking was spreading like a tide across her body. Turner feared she would fall so he instinctively reached his arm around her waist to support her, letting go of her vice-like grip on his hand. Tears rolled freely down her cheeks, and he could see in the gloom that she was pursing her lips tightly and nodding her head back and forward as if trying to keep some level of control.

'Bill, Juliet wants you to know she loves you, and she is sorry she didn't get to say goodbye in this world.' His voice soft in the darkness. 'Please tap three times if you understand this time.' Again another long pause and then tap ... tap ... tap. Juliet was cold to the touch now and seemed to be going into shock. Worried about her health, he quickly continued, 'She wants you to know she says goodbye and hopes you are well on the other side. Please tap twice if you are well and wish also to tell her goodbye and that you love her.' Almost immediately this time there came a tap ... tap – then Juliet fainted into a messy heap onto the floor.

Turner let go of the Bluetooth device he'd been triggering in his pocket. It was linked to a vibration speaker concealed in the base of one of the candles, expertly disguised in its waxy shell. Using different buttons, he could trigger one to four eerie taps whenever he wanted, and it had proved a perfect tool for séances. As he reached down to help the fallen figure of the hotel owner, the TriField meter went off. Swearing at his carelessness for not checking it was switched off before starting the tapping routine, he grabbed it roughly off the fireplace. To his complete surprise, it was, in fact, switched off but the needle was jumping crazily from side to side with the alarm screaming loudly into the blackened room. Turner shook his head and cursed the RADAK Corporation. The 'Remote and Distance Activity Kit' manufacturers were an underground supplier of electronics and other fake equipment to the professional psychic community. Lately they'd been sourcing parts from various dubious Far East factories, and it looked like this faulty behaviour was the result.

Turner felt like he was being watched. The air felt heavy

and cold as if a freezing night fog was slowly seeping into the corners of the darkened room. The screaming meter dropped violently out of his hand and cracked open into a tangled mess of shattered plastic and wiring. He wrinkled his nose as a waft of putrid decay formed around him. The smell of salt, the sea and rotting flesh made him retch violently. Shivering uncontrollably, goose bumps prickling his flesh like tiny needles, he looked down into the fireplace just in time to see the embers fizz and glow then explode into flame. The cold had been replaced with a scorching inferno that reeked of rotten eggs and wood smoke. A crackling, spitting fire raged its way up the chimney causing him to step back almost stumbling over the prone figure of Juliet Armstrong. The flames held his gaze, and he felt compelled to move closer to them until he could sense the blistering heat singeing his prized boots.

Panting desperately, Turner threw himself backwards onto the floor. He could hear something. Above the roar of the flames he could definitely hear something else. He turned his head to the side and listened intently. A scraping hollow voice was saying something. The sound cut through him like fingernails being scraped down a blackboard.

'Turner ... Turner ... ' The words were empty and thin, pushing themselves into his terrified mind. It was a girl's voice, hollow and shrill. 'I ... can ... see ... you ... Turner.' He scrambled desperately to his knees, glaring around the room for the source of the sad lilting tones.

And then it was gone. The lights flicked on in the room, causing him to squint from the sudden glare, and the candle flames guttered out. 'Mrs Armstrong, Mrs Armstrong, can you hear me?' he pleaded, shaking her gently by the shoulders. Slowly she groaned and blinked her eyes before she in turn recoiled from the bright light. Turner raced into the kitchen to get her a glass of water, and by the time he returned she had managed to prop herself up on her elbows. Gratefully accepting the water, he helped her carefully shuffle into one of the other lounge chairs in the room. 'What's that smell?' she asked, wrinkling her nose. The stench of the wood smoke still lingered in the room.

'I think one of the candles must have burnt part of a chair leg. I'm so sorry,' he lied, knowing he couldn't say what had just happened. In truth, he wasn't even sure himself. He was still shaking. Thankfully, she seemed to accept the explanation, then reached out to hold his quivering hand.

'Thank you,' she said, staring him straight in his blue eyes, and hugged him to her. They sat like this, just holding each other, for some minutes before realising that the intimacy seemed inappropriate. As he began to pack away the velvet drapes, handkerchief, candles and shattered meter, she pushed the little black carved box that had so fascinated her husband into his hands. 'Take this. It is too painful for me to keep. Looking at it every day … Please Nathen … Please. I need to move on now. It would really help me let go.' She was pleading with him now.

He simply muttered, 'Of course,' and casually placed it in the leather briefcase. After a final lingering hug, Juliet Armstrong thrust his payment for the evening into his hand and he was off gingerly down the stairs, out into the cool night.

Pausing outside, he looked back at the flat and the streets surrounding it trying to figure out if anyone was around who could have played a trick on him. All he could see was a stray cat slinking around on its nightly prowl, darting in and out of the shadows of the streetlights. The memory of the voice lingered in his mind, and he shook his head vigorously from side to side, trying to clear his thoughts. He stared down at his burnt boots, the peeling snakeskin scales from the toes flaking off in the light breeze. Something had definitely happened but what exactly he couldn't be sure. It was the early hours of the morning and as he headed back through town the last few die-hard partygoers were stumbling through the night, singing and swearing in equal measure. Quickly he made his way back down the narrow cobblestone streets heading towards the railway station and then over the river bridge. All the way home he couldn't get rid of the feeling that someone or something was watching him.

CHAPTER 6

JADE

After a restless night filled with nightmares of hollow voices and flickering flames, Turner woke early in a cold sweat. His sheets were soaked with his clammy perspiration, and the blue cotton bedclothes looked as if they'd been in some sort of linen fight to the death.

Downstairs in the kitchen he found a brief hand-written note on the back of a torn breakfast cereal box in brown felt-tip pen showing Lee's quickly scrawled handwriting:

Bro,
Gone to Newcastle to trade the Strat.
Should be back tomorrow.
Love, peace and bacon grease
Lee & Sandra

'The Strat' was a tobacco sunburst 1978 Fender Stratocaster electric guitar that Lee had bought for peanuts from a second-hand shop in Leeds about a decade earlier. He'd now found out that it was worth a couple of thousand to the right buyer after scanning a recent article in *Guitar Player* magazine. Obviously the right buyer must have come along, if he was willing to head a hundred miles north to sell it. This was how the relationship between Nathen Turner and Lee Melone worked and why it worked so well. They were both free spirits who had shared the best and worst of times together. Their various girlfriends of all shapes and sizes had come and gone but the bond between them never wavered. Lee knew Turner didn't have any psychic gigs for a few days so he'd decided to take off and do his own thing, simple as that. Lee didn't need to ask permission. Even though they only had one car between them, he knew Turner would just make do with walking everywhere – their house was only five minutes from the town centre.

Turner showered and dressed, this time in an outrageously loud red flowered shirt, grabbed the leather briefcase from the night before and headed into town. He walked alongside the busy road that ran parallel to the River Esk before crossing over into Grape Lane. The lane was so narrow and dark at night that the locals called it 'Grope Lane' as it was a favourite haunt of hormonal teenagers looking for a bit of sleazy romance. During the day, it was a busy cramped thoroughfare for the tourists heading out to sample the various fossil hunting, woodcarving, antique and do-it-yourself stores it held. The tall Victorian buildings curved around the corner to the main street, and at the centre of the curve stood The Alchemist, Turner's home from home when Lee was away. The spiritualist shop had been there for as long as he could remember, owned by Kenny and Rosa Florian, two flower-power dropouts who had decided to try to make a living doing what they loved – which was basically as little as possible. Kenny was outside, washing down the small wooden framed windows in his denim dungarees and a torn green T-shirt, his long black hair tied back in a ponytail. 'Bloody seagulls,' he cursed, wiping more of their stinking white waste from the sills. Turner laughed, making Kenny turn to notice him approaching the shop.

'Nate!' he called out, refusing to call him Nathen or Turner as it wasn't cool in hippy speak. 'How's it hanging, dude?'

'Low and loaded,' he replied, smiling back at him, keeping with the hippy vibe.

'Still no girlfriend, eh? We need to get that baby batter in the right place, man, not just the back of your hand.' And so it went on with even more crude jibes before they'd had enough and entered the shop, bent over laughing at each other.

The Alchemist was a small purple-fronted shop selling the usual plethora of tarot cards, candles, New Age books, crystals and the odd ceremonial goblet or two. The interior looked like a blind monkey with a spray can had designed it. Psychedelic greens mixed with bright purple and sunshine yellow in a totally random array. The truth was actually not too far away from this. When Kenny and Rosa took over the store they'd got a little carried away, celebrating with a couple of bottles of Russian vodka, then decided to spray paint it. They actually liked the result, and so it had stayed like this for at least the last two decades. In front of this headache-inducing colour scheme was a random assortment of natural wood shelving made from driftwood salvaged from the beach and carelessly hammered together by Kenny. The payment area had a glass-topped counter containing various talismans with little hand-written cards underneath saying things like 'for good luck' and 'for health'. The place reeked of sandalwood, and Rosa stood smiling happily behind the counter, her crazy bush of unkempt ginger hair giving her a slightly scary look. She was also in dungarees and T-shirt but the front panel of her denim ensemble had a huge yellow rose embroidered over it, covering her tiny breasts. She was puffing happily on a pink electronic cigarette, clouds of vapour rising to form a thin mist under the low ceiling. 'You hungry?' she asked, gesturing at the bubbling pots visible through the open door of the small kitchen area at the back of the shop.

Turner and Kenny smirked at each other. Rosa was always experimenting with new recipes from the Internet, most of which were completely inedible. The 'Field Mushroom Soup' experience from a month ago had left Turner with a minor dose of food poisoning and put him off for life. When he politely answered 'no,' she sulkily shuffled off into the back room to continue tinkering with her latest brew. Turner took out the shattered TriField meter.

'Bloody hell, you met an angry ghost or something?' Kenny turned the mangled wreckage in his hand.

Turner didn't laugh. He wasn't sure how close to the truth the off-hand comment might be. 'No, I … erm dropped it yesterday over at Oswin Hall. You got another one?'

Kenny led Turner upstairs to the small pokey attic room that stored all his electronic gadgets. There were three uneven shelves full of oddly shaped boxes stacked high, one on top of the other. The array of thermal imaging cameras, digital voice recorders, night-vision goggles and the like made it look more like a supply drop for wannabe secret agents. 'Here you go, latest model,' he said, handing over a container about the size of a shoebox. 'It's not "modified", if you know what I mean,' he continued, and gave him a knowing wink.

'How long will it take to get the usual done?' Turner asked, referring to adding his covert switch.

'About two weeks, I reckon. I can ring the RADAK boys this afternoon and check to make sure.' Turner handed over the cash for the meter and the upgrade, said his goodbyes and headed back to the house to pick up the dog.

Kyle was waiting in the kitchen, pacing up and down, his long black and white tail twitching in irritation at finding the house empty when he woke up. He'd been dreaming about chasing cats, and the furry wool blanket that lined his basket had been kicked out onto the wooden floor. As soon as he saw Turner, he pounced on him, knocking him flat and sending the leather briefcase flying into the corner of the room, springing it open in the process. After half a pint of stinking drool was licked all over his owner's face, Kyle seemed satisfied. He bounded backwards, grabbed his brown twisted leather lead from the kitchen counter and looked up expectantly at Turner.

The pair headed across the river bridge and onto the beach that ran up to the West Pier. It was a beautiful day and Turner kicked off his boots, walking barefoot down to the ebbing tideline. The water fizzed and foamed between his toes, and he could taste the dry salt air in his mouth. The air smelt of a combination of newly mown grass and salt, that distinctive tang of the sea. Kyle jumped in and out of the surf, chasing a driftwood stick Turner nonchalantly threw out into the bubbling water for him. He barked loudly before pounding into the waves and paddling like crazy to get to it. They continued this game for over an hour before Kyle was exhausted. Kyle signalled this to his barefoot owner by exiting the sea and shaking himself vigorously right next to him, soaking Turner in sea water, bits of sand and sopping wet green slimy seaweed. They retired to the rocks to dry out and the hairy wet hound settled into a silent and deep slumber at his side.

Looking around, Turner noticed a young couple holding hands and chatting gaily as they paddled up to their ankles in the freezing water. His thoughts turned to Jade, and he wondered what she'd be doing now and whether she would even remember him – he couldn't even remember if he'd told her his name. On an impulse, he pulled out the crumpled piece of yellow paper he'd been carrying in his jeans since they met. Reaching for his phone, he dialled the number, not really knowing what to say but just feeling he needed to talk to her. To his complete surprise, she answered after two rings.

'Jade? Jade, is that you? It's Nathen Turner – loud shirt and terrible artist from the London flight last week.' He could feel his throat tightening with nerves, so he coughed quietly to clear it.

Two hundred and fifty miles away at the other end of the line, Jade was pounding on a treadmill, desperately trying to hear what he was saying over the noise of the clanking gym machines. The call had cut through the music she had piped into the headphones attached to her mobile phone resting in the cup holder between the treadmill's padded front bars. The sweat poured from her, creating a damp dark stain between her breasts on her tight grey T-shirt. As she listened to the music, she continually glanced at the heart-rate monitor on the machine to make sure she was exercising in the right cardio zone. She dreamt of a time when looking good didn't have to be part of the job description. How anybody said they loved working out was beyond her – Jade always despised it. The gym was full of alpha-male city boys looking for an easy lay. For them what happens in London stays in London, and they would all trot off happily at the weekends to the wife and kids after a week of drunken debauchery in the city. They were all there – the brokers, the lawyers, the management consultants ... Porsche driving tossers, as she preferred to call them. She knew this was unfair, but after a disastrous relationship with a banker called Rupert, or 'Ru' to his friends, her resentment was at boiling point. Turns out 'Ru', the fun-loving guy looking for adventure, was actually a middle-aged gentleman who dyed his hair black and had a wife and two kids in Somerset. His wife had found Jade's number on his iPhone under 'Dentist Nurse' and called to check when his next dental appointment was. Wanker.

'Hello, hello, I can't hear you. Hang on a moment,' Jade gasped as she stopped the machine and headed to the quieter area by the changing rooms. This morning gym session was part of her daily routine when she had time off. The rest of it was usually spent between shopping with her girlfriends and catching up with family in Chinatown near London's West End theatre district.

Turner repeated his initial introduction and, to his huge relief, she remembered him. Luckily, the Vegas flight was her last shift before a week off and then she was being moved onto the European circuit covering the Italian routes. The airlines had started doing this to help the crew cope with jet lag – one set of shifts on long haul and the next on short haul and then the pattern repeated. Jade could hear the sound of gulls and the sea behind Turner and asked what it was.

'You ever heard of Dracula?' he asked mischievously. She

said that of course she had. 'Well, I live in his home town.'

'Where? Transylvania? I thought from your accent you lived up north.' In her head, she was seeing visions of flaming castles with angry villagers banging on the door.

'I do live up north,' he said, chuckling at her remark. 'I don't mean where he was born, I mean his hometown in England. It's called Whitby – I'm sitting on the beach on a glorious sunny day, watching the world go by. Just thought I'd give you a call, see if you remember you owe me a drink.' He pressed the phone tightly to his head, listening intently for the reply.

'Of course I remember you. I don't give my number to every passenger I meet,' she said, worried he might think she played fast and loose with many potential boyfriends.

Turner was relieved. 'Well, vampires are a big thing up here. We have a goth festival every year – sort of celebrates everything that is a bit dark and bizarre. There's some great bands …'

She seemed genuinely fascinated and he went on to describe the beach and the town in exciting detail, eager to talk about the place he loved most in the world. Unwittingly, he was doing a better job than the best efforts of the Whitby Tourist Board. He asked about her American accent and she explained that her family had moved from Japan to Austin, Texas, when she was only eight to follow her father's engineering job in the oil industry. Just after she'd graduated from high school, they moved to London after her father accepted an offer he couldn't refuse from British Petroleum. With no friends in London at the time and a wicked sense of adventure, she'd earned her wings as an air stewardess by the time she was twenty and set off to travel the world.

On they talked for more than half an hour, laughing and enjoying each other's stories. He was relieved that she never asked him what he did so he wasn't forced to break the mood of the light conversation with tales about his psychic leanings. He'd moved on to Lee and how he'd headed north on his guitar version of the *Antiques Roadshow*.

'Does that mean you've got a spare bed?' Before he had time to think he blurted out that he most definitely had, and she was welcome to visit any time. He was trying to be polite but nearly dropped the phone at her next remark.

'Great! I'm on my way – give me directions from the motorway …' she said in a matter-of-fact way that took him completely by surprise. Her constant impulsive behaviour had earned her the family nickname of 'Wild Spirit'. For Jade, life was for living, and she approached each day as if it were her last. Her father put it down to some renegade bloodline buried deep in their family history and now untraceable. Her typical devil-may-care rash behaviour and green eyes were most certainly not Japanese.

Turner's heart was literally skipping a beat when he came off the phone. With a rush of adrenalin and sheer excitement, he punched the air, making the dog wonder sleepily what the hell was going on. The next thing he felt was panic. There was no food in the house and Lee's room looked and smelled like a bear had been camping in it for a week. Pushing on his boots, he dragged the docile dog onto its feet as he scrambled for the nearest grocery store.

Two hours later, he'd stocked up on fresh vegetables and chicken, ready to make a stir-fry for their evening meal. He vainly hoped his Asian culinary expertise would impress Jade. Not sure which alcohol to get, he had played safe with red and white wine, beer, lager, vodka and rum. If things didn't go well at least he could drown his sorrows. Lee's room had been sprayed, wiped and cleaned with an obsessive attention to detail that would put the best hospital to shame.

The phone rang and his heart dropped as he wondered whether she was calling to cancel.

'Nate? Its Kenny.' He let out a sigh of relief. 'You know that broken TriField meter of yours? Well I took it apart this afternoon to see if I could salvage anything for spares. I've never seen anything like it – everything inside is melted and fused together. What the hell did you drop it on?'

Downstairs in the kitchen, Turner's discarded leather briefcase began to make a dull scraping and tapping noise as if somebody or something was trying to crawl out. Inside the bag lay the carved black box he'd been given the night before. The sounds seemed to be coming from inside the box.

The scratching and scraping got louder. Kyle woke from his slumber on the other side of the room, tilted his large furry head and pricked up his ears. Stretching and yawning, in the totally non-self-conscious way dogs do, he padded slowly across the room, his claws clip-clopping on the wooden floor. With nose poked curiously inside the open briefcase, he snuffled deep into the soft cotton lining looking for the source of the noise.

Eventually his damp snout touched against the deep carving on the box lid. His sensitive nose could feel that something inside was definitely moving. Gently, he opened his jaws and grabbed the curious package, trying to drag it out between his yellowing canines. It took him four goes and a bit of deft manoeuvring with his shaggy paws before it spun and slid across the floor like a cork being released from a flat bottle of champagne. Carefully he cowered back, cocking his head again to listen for the noises. Something smelt wrong. Then he felt as if an icy hand was grabbing at the thick fur around his neck and choking him. In sheer panic, he let out a piercing howl.

The shrill wailing sent a shiver of fear through Turner. He dropped the phone and bounded downstairs. Kyle was lying motionless on his side, tongue lolling wetly from his mouth, dark eyes staring into space. Blood was dripping thickly from his nose, making a slick red puddle on the floor. The room smelt of decay and rotting flesh, and his panting breath was puffing clouds of mist into the freezing air. Turner began to tremble uncontrollably.

Then he heard it – a hollow clawing, grating echo that rasped through the icy air. Scanning the room, he could only see his briefcase dragged half way across the kitchen and most of its contents spewed carelessly across the floor. The brass catches were stained with blood.

'Bloody dog,' he muttered into the air, assuming the renegade pooch had injured himself trying to scavenge for food in his briefcase. Trying to hold back the feeling of panic growing inside him, he quickly threw everything back in the briefcase. For some reason the little carved box that was next to Kyle felt icy cold to his touch. Too worried about the dog to pay the box much attention, he carelessly flipped it inside and then stuffed the briefcase into the cupboard under the sink.

Kyle was starting to move a little so Turner grabbed a

towel and cleaned him up. Instinctively he reached for the kettle. Tea would calm his shattered nerves, he thought. Tipping the dried jasmine green tea leaves into his cup and pouring on the steaming water, he said, 'Bloody hell,' to no one in particular, the cold sweat running down his face.

CHAPTER 7

TERROR IN THE NIGHT

The fragrant tea did settle Turner's nerves, but the dog spent the rest of the afternoon moping in the corner, occasionally looking up and listening intently. By now Jade should be well on her way, so he tried to make himself busy doing things – anything to take his mind off the growing fear that was gnawing at his soul. Something wasn't right; he knew that. Maybe he'd underestimated the effect of the jet lag this time. He just couldn't get past the feeling that weird things were happening around him. Constant glancing for movements in the shadows and bouts of unexplained shivering were not helping to calm his anxiety.

So he ironed. Shirts, socks, underwear, jeans – anything that would make him concentrate on something mundane and keep his shaking hands occupied. To lighten the mood he brought the MP3 player down from the lounge and sat it on a kitchen shelf, blaring out all his blues favourites. Like Lee, he had just connected with blues music from the very first time he'd heard it; he could feel it in his bones. He was singing loudly and badly along with T-Bone Walker, nodding and bobbing his head to 'Call It Stormy Monday' when there was a gentle tapping at the kitchen door (which also happened to be the front door of the house). The dog was still sulking and didn't even move. Turner peeled open the heavy oak door in the fading evening light to find Jade beaming at him from the roadway, leaning on the top of her red Mini Cooper. The pose emphasised the curve of her beautiful hips, and the tight butt contained within skinny black denim jeans. A low-cut billowing dark-green silk blouse was tucked tightly into the waistband, the thin fabric gently pushing against her breasts. The whole image was simply stunning, and she was way more beautiful than he remembered. Jade threw the small bag she was carrying at him, locked the car and trotted daintily up and gave him a kiss on the cheek.

'Wow, this is so cool,' she clucked happily, turning around to look at the fading sun silhouetting the fishing boats in the harbour. Turner was still fumbling desperately, trying to cling onto the bag she'd thrown at him after his catch had been slightly mistimed. Laughing at him juggling the bag, she pushed past into the kitchen with its jumble of assorted clothing hanging around the ironing board. The dog looked up from his corner and started to wag his tail. Turner watched in amazement as his hound, the leaping frothing 'bowl you over at the door' canine, calmly trotted up and then, after a quick sniff, gently licked her hand. Jade laughed again at his surprised expression as he stumbled in and closed the door behind him. She had a real presence, like a bolt of electricity lighting up the room, and he felt like a moth fluttering into the glow of her alluring flame. Her hips were moving sexily to the slow blues tunes. 'I love this music … reminds me of my childhood,' she said, closing her eyes.

He raised an eyebrow and was about to ask how a Japanese siren knew about blues when she saved him the trouble. 'Where I went to high school, they had a blues club that we'd sneak off to at night to join in the dancing, just letting the live tunes wash over us. It was so neat – Antone's Club was the place to be, man. I loved it.' Her American accent got stronger as the memories of the smoky club came back to her. Talking with Jade just cleansed his mind; her beauty overpowered him. When she looked at him with those deep green eyes, he felt all the worry of the previous evening just wash away.

By the time Turner had snapped out of his lovesick fawning she was halfway up the stairs. 'What's up here?' she asked enthusiastically before bounding up without waiting for an answer. Gladly he followed her bouncing bum up to the lounge on the first floor. She headed straight for the window and gazed out across the harbour mouth, the evening lights flicking on in the fading gloom. Still looking outside she grabbed his hand and gasped, 'This is amazing! What a fantastic view.' The dry warmth of her touch excited him, and he just nodded in agreement. They stood in silence, gazing out at the West Pier and watching the tiny figures going about their business totally oblivious to the two watchers at the window.

Then she was off again, bounding up the stairs to the second floor with him chasing breathlessly behind her. 'This is your room,' he panted, opening Lee's sanitised and scrubbed emporium, 'and I'm upstairs. The bathroom and shower are just here if you want to freshen up after the trip. Just make yourself at home.' Jade jumped on Lee's bed with an excited giggle and gazed around the room. Fading yellow Hep Cats posters were stuck randomly to the wall and there were CDs everywhere, tottering towers of them in every corner. Three guitars hung on the long wall opposite the bed and a black amplifier, appropriately labelled 'Boogie', sat underneath them with leads coiled neatly on the floor.

'Shower sounds great. Get some of that London smog off me.' Jade sounded happy and was flicking through a pile of CDs, admiring the collection. Turner grabbed her a clean towel and headed back down to start on the meal. He felt really comfortable, just like he'd known her all his life. Whistling gaily, he started slicing and dicing the vegetables, his feelings of unease now a long-distant memory.

Back upstairs, Jade was getting bolder in her exploration of her new surroundings and pulled open Lee's wardrobe to find an array of beach clothes and casual jeans – she couldn't spot a suit or tie anywhere. Sandra's side was much the same with the addition of a range of lacy see-through underwear, and Jade couldn't resist feeling the soft texture and rubbing it between her fingers. Turning, she cheekily strummed one of the guitars before returning to her musical review of the CDs stacked next to the amp. They read like a blues catalogue all the way from Blind Lemon Jefferson to Jimi Hendrix. She was impressed and very relieved – no signs she'd come to stay with some weirdo axe murderer. It had been a risk inviting herself to a stranger's house, but he seemed safe enough so far. Her investigation ended on the small cabinet next to the bed that bizarrely had a half-eaten bowl of peanuts and an ashtray sitting on the top. Shrugging silently she opened the top drawer and let out a shocked giggle. It was full of various shapes and sizes of sex toys. She closed it quickly, feeling slightly embarrassed, and headed for the shower. So far, her trip north was proving more than interesting.

Half an hour later, Jade padded down into the kitchen with hair still damp to see Turner expertly flipping a wok over the gas hob. The smell was fabulous; a mixture of ginger, garlic and chilli aromas floated across the room, and she inhaled deeply, drinking it all in like a fine wine. The ironing was gone and the table was set for two with black lacquered chopsticks laid carefully at each side. Bowls of soy sauce and a peanut dip were in the exact centre, with a large empty crystal wine goblet each side. To the right of the table, a range of drinks were arranged in size order on the windowsill, with wine and spirits on the left and beers on the right. The sound of her bare footsteps on the wood floor made him turn, and he almost lost control of the pan when he saw what she was wearing. Jade's long black hair hung to her shoulders, perfectly framing her oval face. She was dressed in a light blue kimono-style top, tied with a thin black silk belt. The kimono top ended high at the curve of her thighs, covering a short black tight skirt. Her long beautiful legs and bare feet completed the look, her toes topped with glossy blue varnish.

'Do you like it?' she said, twirling around to give him a better look. 'In Japan we call this type of top a "Happi Coat" and we usually wear them for festivals and parties – seemed appropriate somehow.' Her eyes stared directly into his as she asked and the best he could do was, 'Y … Y … Yes, it looks fabulous,' before going bright red and turning back to the stove. Laughing again, she grabbed a bottle of white wine off the sill and poured them both a large glass. Turner accepted gratefully and downed it in one, causing her gentle tinkling giggle to fill the room once more.

They talked like old friends over the food, greedily munching through Turner's expert meal and working their way down through the row of drinks on the windowsill, which now stood half empty. He had never felt so relaxed with a woman before; she was so easy to talk to and didn't take herself, or life, too seriously. Long into the night they swapped stories and life experiences, immersed in each other's company. It was so refreshing for Turner not to have to resort to his usual manipulation techniques to make headway with a woman. He discussed what he did in roundabout terms as a party planner and organiser for various types of spiritual events, and she seemed satisfied with that. Even Kyle could sense the happy mood as he trotted from one to the other under the table, gladly taking the titbits they offered.

Jade chattered with enthusiasm and was just reaching the end of another of her long Texas tales when the soft sound of Turner's snoring made her glance up from stroking Kyle. He'd nodded off in a drunken haze and she giggled silently to herself, amused by his inability to hold his liquor. Swiftly, she tidied the kitchen and put everything in the dishwasher before hauling him to his feet and manoeuvring his lanky legs towards the stairs. Slowly, she coaxed his thin drunken frame up the three flights and levered him onto his bed, Kyle curling up happily at his feet.

After closing the door softly, she headed down to her room and flopped into a deep sleep, still dressed in the short kimono jacket and black skirt, finally giving in to the effects of the large meal and boozy conversation. A few hours later, her mouth felt like it had been roughly sandblasted, and her dry tongue was swollen and sore. She woke up coughing, desperately needing water. The pounding inside her head made her reel but she carefully pushed to the edge of the bed and put her feet on the floor. Stumbling in the dark, feeling her way to the door, she cursed as her foot kicked over one of Lee's CD piles en route.

The pale blue glow of the moon coming through the landing window was blinding in comparison with the darkness of the room, softly illuminating her way down the stairs into the kitchen. She fumbled for the light switch and flicked it on. The sudden glare made her wince and swear under her breath. Grasping the kitchen counter for security, she tottered slowly to the sink. Pouring a large mug of cold water right up to the brim, she eagerly gulped it down. The fresh liquid was heaven. The sweet nectar soothed her shrivelled palette as she loudly gargled before letting it glide down her crusty throat.

In the dead silence of the moonlit night, a muffled tapping and scraping noise echoed from under the sink. Perhaps she'd dripped some of the water down the back of the unit, she thought. Opening the cupboard door to investigate, a sudden odour of rotting flesh made her gag and grasp at her throat. 'What the hell?' She pulled out the leather briefcase Turner had tossed in earlier, then pushed it at arm's length onto the kitchen table. The stench was coming from the bag.

With her nose wrinkled in disgust, she dumped the contents carelessly onto the table, searching for the source of the revolting smell. She felt cold. The bitter chill thrust through her body like an icy harpoon, making her shiver and tremble uncontrollably. Without warning a scratching and scraping sound enveloped the room, hitting her fuzzy senses from every direction at once. There was something about the sound that wasn't natural, like bloody hands crawling through grave dirt. Instinctively, she pulled her rumpled kimono coat tightly around her.

'I ... see ... you,' a hollow rasping voice hissed from

directly behind her. Jade whirled around to see a naked young Asian girl standing at the foot of the stairs. Moonlight formed an ethereal glow around her bony figure, making the back of the spectre's dark hair shimmer brightly in the gloom. The frail milky white spirit was a grotesque mess of oozing red wounds with frightening black hollows where the eyes used to be. The horrible black voids were staring at her as if seeing into her very soul.

Jade rubbed her face vigorously, trying to clear her head. She must be imagining things; maybe it was just a combination of too much alcohol and not enough sleep. Her fingers pinched her arm violently, trying to wake herself from the horrific nightmare. Letting out a painful yelp from the nip, she realised she was awake and this was very real. There was something about the ghoulish apparition that reminded her of the past, maybe some dark fairy tale from her childhood. The face was a distorted mess of swollen putrid sores, the hair lank and wet as the terrifying figure stood staring straight at her.

Then it smiled. Yellow rotting teeth dripped more thick blood. Slowly, it was gliding across the frigid room, arms outstretched, clawing at the air, inching their way forward.

With a monstrous terrified wail, Jade tried to run, but the figure was blocking her path back upstairs, and the kitchen door was locked. Gasping desperately for breath she slumped heavily to the floor; sinking into blackness, she knew no more.

CHAPTER 8

THE KEEPER OF THE WATCH

The Sunday lunchtime service at the Oswin Hall Hotel seemed slower than usual. James Roby looked around impatiently for the waiter, tapping his calloused hands on the white tablecloth. He only had an hour before he was due back at work, and he liked to be fed and watered well before heading into his long tiring evening shift as the harbour watchkeeper. He was not the most patient of men.

Ever since his wife passed away from a long and painful struggle with multiple sclerosis, he'd been coming here every Sunday. He'd done his best to be a carer, financial provider and listening ear when she was depressed but, in the end, it just ground him down, watching her body gradually shut down as the myelin protecting her nervous system was eaten away by the disease. When it attacked her respiratory system, he knew it was the end. The doctor and nurses tried their best but still couldn't prevent pneumonia setting into the weakening tissue. She'd died in his arms, at home, as she wanted to, leaving him alone and incredibly resentful of the cards life had dealt him.

Now the resentment and anger fuelled his days, making him short tempered and intolerant of most others, except his best friend Ross Pearson. They'd served together in the British merchant navy after being roommates at *HMS Copley*, the impressive training college housed in a converted shipwreck on the banks of the Menai Strait in North Wales. Joining the

Blue Funnel Line as indentured cadets, together they qualified as professional engineers some years later. He'd never wanted to be an engineer, preferring the more glamorous life and salary of a deck officer, but he'd failed his eyesight colour test so was deemed medically unfit to do the role. For him, this was how his cursed life went – whenever he wanted or longed for something, he could never get it. The unfairness of life burnt into his soul and the only way he knew how to express the pain was through violence and rage. In this, he and Pearson were like peas in a pod. As the son of an abusive alcoholic father who beat him every chance he got, Pearson had plenty of fire in his belly that needed to be vented on the world.

This had first become apparent when they headed out on shore leave together in Hong Kong as young men. They were working on the clean and efficient 12,000-ton MV Glendale, covering the Ceylon, Singapore, Bangkok and Yokohama route. The ship was a fairly modern design at the time, with air-conditioned cabins and all the latest mod cons. It was comfortable and easy to maintain – too easy as far as the two engineering pals were concerned, as it needed less time in port than the others in the fleet. The short time ashore usually forced them to cram their drinking and rebel-rousing into a twenty-four hour period, most of which they would never remember the next day. On the first occasion in Hong Kong, they'd taken the boat taxi to the Liberty floating restaurant, pushing cautiously past the crowded wooden junks bobbing in the harbour. Stomachs fit to bursting with Chinese food, they'd then headed to Neptune's Bar on a kamikaze-driven rickshaw through the jammed streets, determined to drink their weight in beer and spirits. Five hours and twenty drinks later, they could hardly see straight and headed onto the sidewalk to grab a return rickshaw ride back to the ship. A drab tramp dressed in grey rags approached them from one of the narrow alleys nearby. His rank smell filled the street as he knelt down and reached out his bony hands in a begging gesture, swaying silently back and forward. Without warning, Roby made a drunken violent lunge, kicking him square in the chest, causing squeals of pain as the quivering retch cowered away terrified. Enjoying the power of the moment, Pearson joined in, laughing as they both hammered blows into the helpless figure. So started the pattern of food, alcohol and violence that stayed with them for the rest of their naval career.

Roby deftly grabbed hold of a passing waiter by the bottom of his waistcoat. 'Where's my bloody food?' he barked gruffly.

'I'll check, Mr Roby, very sorry for the delay,' said the waiter, scrambling off towards the kitchen like the hounds of hell were after him. All the staff knew Roby and he terrified them with his rough and ready ways. All, that is, except for Oswin Hall's owner Juliet Armstrong, who had seen many of his type before and knew exactly how to handle them.

After a delay of around five minutes, Juliet walked slowly and purposefully out of the kitchen, carrying a tray towards his regular single table in the corner of the oak-beamed restaurant. Dressed shabbily in a loose dress and white apron, she looked like she hadn't slept all night. With a shallow smile she placed a steaming plate of belly pork, black pudding and apple mash delicately in front of him. 'There's your lunch, Mr Roby. I've had a bit of an eventful night so we're running a little late today. Sorry for your wait.' She smiled into his eyes before leaning forward to whisper into his ear, 'And if you touch one of my staff again I'll cut your bloody balls off with a blunt knife! If you don't like the service, you can leave now.' Still smiling, she took a step back from the table, her eyes this time boring straight into his.

This was language Roby could understand, and he respected Juliet Armstrong for defending her establishment. The insult made him bark with laughter, and he nodded and mouthed sorry meekly before blitzing his meal with a blanket of salt and strong pepper and diving in like a ravenous wolf. Satisfied, Juliet turned and swept through the rest of the diners, offering her apologies for the tardiness of the service and reassuring everybody that their meals were on the way. Her presence seemed to make the whole of the restaurant relax and the muttered disquiet turned back to polite conversation and giggling laughter.

Things seemed to go smoothly after that, with meal upon meal rushing from the bustling kitchen, gratefully received by the seated guests. The restaurant was thinning out, with only a couple of people left including Roby. He leant back content in his chair and spooned three sugars into his black coffee. The caffeine and energy boost they provided would be most welcome to help get him through his afternoon shift. Juliet arrived to clean up and hovered around busily, collecting cutlery and dirty plates.

'Rough night, huh?' he stated rather than asked, seeing her unkempt hair and smudged make up.

'You could say that. I talked to Bill ...' As soon as the words were out of her mouth Roby gagged on his coffee in disbelief and leant across the table, clamping her wrist to the tablecloth.

'But he's dead, isn't he? How the hell could you talk to him?' he said in complete shock.

'Through a psychic. I've used him before – a lot of us have,' she replied, sweeping her hand around the room to include her staff in the statement. 'He's really good and has helped me a lot with things in the past. We used one of Bill's favourite things to call him back, just for a brief time. The psychic said it would form a bridge between our world and his. Apparently, we all leave a bit of our energy in objects we care about.' Roby sat back wide eyed and open mouthed as she told him the tale of the previous evening and how she had fainted at the end. His long unfulfilled existence had made him very superstitious as he looked in vain for various causes of his continued bad luck. Over the years, he'd collected a string of charms and talismans that were alleged to bring good fortune into the life of the owner. Hence, rather than with scepticism, he viewed Juliet's story with sheer fascination and also a little fear.

He asked more and more about the evening, astonishing Juliet with his polite questioning rather than his usual direct interrogation technique. When she told him more about how they'd used the carved wooden box, his questioning became more intense.

'Does this box have any kind of recognisable design on it at all?' He was leaning over, watching her reaction closely.

'Yes, as a matter of fact it does. How did you know?' she said, curious about his question. 'It's one of those curly pagan patterns – I think they call it a Celtic knot or cross on the lid and more carving on the sides. The weird thing is, it rattles when it's empty. Never could understand it. Anyway, why are you so interested?'

'Well, it's nothing really. Just …' He hesitated mid sentence as if thinking, 'I sort of collect good-luck tokens and stuff like that. I was wondering if it was like some of them I have, that's all.' The colour had drained from his face, and he was fidgeting nervously with his coffee cup.

Juliet knew about the mariner's superstitious collection so thought no more about it. 'Look, we're closing soon. I've got to go.' As she moved away from the table, Roby grabbed her apron.

'Can I talk to you later? I finish around ten. Please – I'd really like to hear more about what happened. Ever since my wife died I've been interested in trying to contact her.' Juliet pulled angrily out of his grip, not buying this excuse. As far as she remembered, he'd been out drinking every day since his wife passed on, and she was getting fed up with his constant questioning.

'Get the hell off me. I think we've talked enough, don't you? Now go. I've got to close up.' With that she was off, heading back to the kitchen.

Roby left Oswin Hall, hurried down the narrow street, across the busy road and skirted past the large Tourist Information Centre on his way to the harbour master's office. Looking around carefully, he stopped at the huge wrought-iron entrance gate and pulled out his phone. Checking he couldn't be overhead, he quickly dialled the local number he knew so well.

'Boss, that you?' he almost whispered into the handset. 'I think we've got a problem. You know your box – the black one with the carvings you gave that Asian girl. I think it's still around. Sounds like it's turned up at Oswin Hall.'

'Come on, that was twenty years ago; it can't be the same one. You told me you'd cleared all traces from that goth slut's room – like she'd just packed up and left. You telling me you didn't? It's a bit bloody late now!' The voice was frustrated, not accepting Roby's story.

'We never found the box in her room. You remember, right?' The voice went quiet at the other end of the line then started cursing loudly. Roby pressed on, 'Look, I don't know, OK? It just seems too much of a coincidence to have two like that kicking around in Whitby. It has to be the same one. Anyway, it's not empty – it's rattling. She must have put something in the hidden compartment. Maybe it's nothing but …' He left the comment hanging.

'She never had anything of mine …' The line went deathly quiet for a few seconds. 'Shit! The note – we never found the other half of the note I gave her. Can't be, it's impossible after all this time. No one is even looking for her anymore.'

The voice went quiet again, thinking desperately about the possible consequences of the discovery. Finally, spoken nervously this time, it said, 'I can't get involved in this; I'd have to make it official and people would start asking questions. She's still on the missing-persons list and this could rake up a shit storm for all of us. You go down to Oswin Hall and find out how they got the box. Where they found it. Just see if they know anything about the girl and her connection with it. Then buy it – whatever it takes, just get it. We need to find if she put my bloody note inside. Take Pearson with you; he's got as much to lose as we have. Let me know when it's done.' The line went dead.

CHAPTER 9

BEER AND CONVERSATION

That evening, the bar at Oswin Hall Hotel was packed full with all ages, shapes and sizes of humanity drinking their collective health.

Around the dimly lit interior, different factions had camped out in separate parts of the dark oak-lined room. The trendy teens were the easiest to identify as they were the loudest and had the most ridiculous haircuts, trying to be cool and fit in with the latest celebrity craze. They clucked and gestured, mirroring the swagger of the rap artists. The boys' trousers hung low, showing off colourful branded boxer-short waistbands underneath. Next came the middle-aged couples dressed in smart casual clothes, looking like they were ready for a golf-club dinner. The men ignored their partners in favour of a detailed discussion on football and local business scandal with other men. Their female companions, likewise, huddled together, talking in hushed tones about how awful their men were before going on to giggle about juicy local sex scandals and the latest *Cosmopolitan* magazine poll results on the subject. Then came the jaded pre-retirement 'what have I wasted my life doing' group steadily drinking themselves depressed, followed by the post retirement 'please don't let me die yet' power drinkers telling tales of their youthful shenanigans.

Amidst this bubbling throng, James Roby and Ross

Pearson sat inconspicuously at the end of the bar, talking quietly back and forth. Roby was tired after his harbour watch shift, but he knew that not carrying out the wishes of the arrogant voice on the phone was unthinkable. The consequences for all of them, including Pearson, could mean humiliation and prison. Hopefully, he'd got it wrong about the carved box and he was worrying about nothing.

'I tell you, Robbo, she doesn't know anything,' Pearson said quietly using Roby's navy nickname. 'She can't do; there's nothing to find.'

'Keep your bloody voice down. If there's nothing to find, how come she has the girl's stupid box, then? We never found it when we cleared the room, remember,' Roby said gruffly over the top of his pint to mask his lip movements.

They were both big strong men with thick necks and muscular physiques forged from years of hard labour at sea. In their day, finding good 'greasers', the slang name for the below-deck crew, willing to do the physical work on the ship's engines and loading systems was nigh on impossible. Most of the best Indian crew who normally did the work had been placed on the ships that were harder to maintain, and Roby and Pearson had been left with the dregs, most of whom didn't want to be there. So they'd done it themselves with a little help from the keener Malay deck crew, and in the process become extremely fit. Roby, as usual, had the sleeves of his red checked wool shirt rolled up, exposing his bulky forearms and navy tattoo. Pearson was dressed in a smart black leather jacket and black polo shirt as he'd had time to change from his day job working on his crab and lobster boat. He still stunk of fish and the sea – the smell never seemed to leave him no matter how hard he scrubbed.

'Can I get you another drink, gentlemen?' Juliet Armstong asked pleasantly from behind the bar. As she delivered another two pints of creamy Guinness to their eagerly waiting arms, Roby leaned in and asked again as nicely as his gruff voice was capable of about the events of the previous night. He was forced to use the excuse that Pearson didn't believe him and wanted to hear it first hand as she was a very reluctant to talk about it after her lunchtime interrogation. Juliet had certainly pulled herself around from her dishevelled appearance earlier. Well-groomed hair framed perfectly applied makeup and she had dressed provocatively in a low-cut red top and tight skirt that was drawing appreciative looks from the faction of middle-aged men. Roby wondered whether this was her way of regaining some of her self-confidence and normal lust for life after the tragic events. Begrudgingly, her words repeated the story of the séance to Pearson, who listened intently and then began to ask carefully worded questions about the carved box they'd used. Where was it found, who did it belong to, had she met the owner? On and on he went until she grew weary of the probing.

She told them what she'd told Lee in the flat two days earlier – it belonged to a young Asian student who'd come for the goth festival a long time ago and left in a hurry. The box was found tucked away behind the headboard of the bed by a cleaner making the room up for the next guest. There was no forwarding address for the girl, so they just kept it and her husband had become intrigued because it rattled when it was empty.

Both men looked at each other and nodded slightly. This

sounded exactly like the incriminating box they were looking for, but they needed to double check. 'What was the girl's name? The goth girl who had the room?' Pearson asked, leaning forward nervously, grabbing his pint to steady his shaking hand.

'How the hell can I remember. It was bloody ages ago!' She was irritated now at the continuing bombardment of questions. 'I'd have to look in the office for that. But who cares? My husband's dead, you moron! Who cares about some stupid bloody box?' She was angry and insulted by these two louts who seemed oblivious to the pain of her recent loss. Impatiently she asked them to drink up and headed down the bar to ring the bell to announce closing time.

The bar cleared quickly and she dimmed the lights and bolted the front door. Juliet was feeling a little more like herself but the loss of her husband still ached inside her. Exhausted and a little light-headed, she pulled down one of the stools that had been stacked on the bar by the cleaner and slouched down. Her staff had left and she'd held back, not really wanting to go home to the empty maisonette.

The front door rattled on its hinges. Someone was urgently hammering on the thick wood, trying to get her attention. She pushed up from her seat and walked tiredly to the door to get rid of whoever it was.

'We're closed,' she shouted through the door.

'Juliet, I'm really sorry. I've left my phone.' She recognised the deep gruff voice of Roby.

'Then get it tomorrow – we're closed,' she repeated more impatiently this time.

'I can't – I need it for work. I'm really sorry.' Roby was

doing his best to sound apologetic.

Reluctantly, she opened the door and scowled at him. 'Hurry up,' she barked as his bulky frame entered into the bar. He looked different. Then she got it – he was wearing black leather gloves and seemed a little nervous. Just as this was going through her head, she felt something push at the back of one of her knees, causing her to crouch as a large gloved hand covered her mouth and nose, pulling her head back sharply and blocking off her air supply. Pearson was holding her tight against him as Roby swung quickly behind and bolted the front door.

'Now, let's finish our nice conversation, shall we?' spat Roby, moving his face to within inches of hers. The façade of polite conversation now gone, he was in full intimidation mode and loving it.

Pearson licked his lips. This was his kind of party. They'd already agreed how to handle things if they couldn't get what they needed from Juliet by 'polite' conversation. Roby slowly reached up his large hands and wrapped them around her throat, guiding her back onto the barstool. Slowly and steadily he pressed into the soft flesh, feeling the cords in her neck resisting him. He loved the sensation under his gloved fingers and continued to tighten his grip. Juliet's lips were blue, and she was gagging, desperate for air. Roby leant forward and spoke menacingly in her ear.

'How's your memory now, eh? What was the name of the girl who stayed in the room where the box was found? Just so we don't misunderstand each other … ' The last words were almost spat at her as he increased the pressure on her throat.

Slowly he eased his grip, and she lolled forwards, gasping

and panting. 'You'll never get away with this, you bastards. Let me go or I'm calling the police.'

'How are you going to do that, Juliet? With your dainty little fingers perhaps.' Roby nodded at Pearson, who removed a short copper pipe from the top of his boot. Pearson slid the pipe over the little finger of her left hand and grabbed the wrist. Slowly, he pulled back on the pipe. There was a sickening crack as the bones splintered near the knuckle. Juliet was trying to scream, but Roby had covered her mouth and was pressing down heavily on her throat again with the other hand.

'Let's try again. You scream, we'll hurt you, much worse this time. Now answer me, who was she?' Roby's face was red with fury, his eyes boring fiercely into hers.

'I don't know. I can't remember. Look in the registers … I don't know … it must have been around late 1994 … I can't really remember exactly … try September that's when the goth festival is …' she was sobbing desperately, repeating her gasping phrases in her panic. 'They're over there … the registers … behind the counter.'

Juliet was gesturing with her good hand towards the hotel entrance and reception desk. Pearson made his way behind the curved counter and pulled out the green folder labelled '1994'. Flicking quickly through the pages of September, he let out a simple cry of 'Got it,' before opening his penknife and carefully cutting out the sheet he wanted.

'See, it wasn't that hard, was it? Now just give me the carved box like a good little girl, and we'll be on our way.' Roby's eyes were red with rage but there was also another emotion there. Pleasure – he was beginning to enjoy himself, invigorated by the power he felt.

'I haven't got it.' Juliet's throat was burning, and the words came out as a hoarse whisper. Her windpipe was collapsing and she could barely breathe.

Roby pressed her throat again, harder this time until she almost blacked out. 'What do you mean, you haven't got it? Where the hell is it?'

'Card … card … in my purse. White card … there …' she gasped, the words struggling out of her sagging frame.

Pearson grabbed her handbag off the bar counter and fished out her purse. It was full of dog-eared family pictures, thirty pounds in change and the usual plethora of bankcards. He pushed it into her good hand. Desperately she fumbled through the inside pockets.

'Here,' she said, raising the white business card up to Roby, 'he has it.' Her head slumped forward heavily onto Roby's gloved hands.

'Who the hell is Nathen Turner? Psychic medium? You've got to be kidding me – not that fool you used last night?' In his frustration he had forgotten his hands were still squeezing her neck. Juliet had stopped moving.

'You've killed her; you bloody idiot!' Pearson snarled at him. 'What the hell do we do now?'

CHAPTER 10

CONFUSION AND KAMI

A bemused Lee Melone knelt over the prone body of a beautiful Japanese lady who lay spreadeagled on his kitchen floor. His bedraggled clothing stunk of cigar smoke from his early-morning drive down from Newcastle with Sandra. He had forgotten the can of Red Bull energy drink he held in his hand – his fourth that morning since they'd left at dawn to avoid the rush-hour traffic. As the journey had only taken them an hour and a half, he was extremely high on the caffeine and sugars from the drink, and was twitching incessantly.

'Where the hell are Nathen and Kyle?' he wondered out loud as Sandra headed quickly up the stairs, shouting their names.

Gently shaking the shoulder of the unconscious figure was having no effect so he decided to blow on her face. To his caffeine-wired mind, this seemed like a really good idea and Sandra returned empty-handed to find him with his lips pursed and almost whistling in Jade's ear.

'What the hell are you doing?' she laughed at him, surveying the bizarre scene. His trembling pupils stared back at her and he burst out laughing as well, realising how stupid he must look.

'He's not in the lounge,' Sandra said in a matter-of-fact way, 'so I'm going to keep looking upstairs, OK?' Without waiting for an answer she was off again up the stairs.

Jade's nose wrinkled at the stale stench of Lee close to her face. She slowly opened her eyes to see this twitching, unkempt man with something held in his hand above her head and screamed loudly. Lee jumped up in fright and rammed his back against the kitchen counter, holding it tightly with his empty hand to keep himself upright. Jade took a closer look at him and realised the object in his hand was a can of Red Bull, and he seemed to be shaking uncontrollably, terrified of her. Recognition set in from the Hep Cats posters she'd seen in the bedroom, and slowly she inched herself up onto her elbows.

'You must be Lee. Where's Nathen?' she asked groggily, her head aching from the drop to the floor and the alcohol from the previous evening.

With perfect timing, Sandra led a very sleepy Nathen Turner carefully down the stairs. He emerged slowly, like a man walking underwater wearing huge leaden shoes. Still dressed in the same clothes from last night, he smelt a little funky from his lack of a clean-up. Squinting painfully at the early-morning light streaming into the kitchen, Turner's mouth tasted like an unwashed hamster had been using it as a toilet. Seeing Jade lying on the floor, he staggered as best he could over to her side.

'You OK? What happened? How did I get to bed?' He had no memory after the end of the last of her Texan stories. Kyle padded cautiously into the room and started wagging his tail as soon as he saw Lee.

'No, Kyle, no …' Lee pleaded but too late. The dog had bounded the short distance to where he stood, jumped up and knocked him flying. Kyle was now straddled over Lee, licking his face enthusiastically, his tail rapidly swishing from side to side.

Infectious laughter rippled around the room. Turner comically introduced Jade, saying he hoped they'd appreciated the traditional Japanese greeting of 'playing dead on a stranger's floor'. They laughed again and gathered happily around the kitchen table cluttered with the contents of the Gladstone briefcase, Lee's shaking causing him to spend an inordinate amount of time trying to put down the can in his hand quietly without spilling it. Sandra made drinks – strong black coffee for her, decaffeinated for Lee and jasmine tea for Turner and Jade.

'Kami,' whispered Jade to nobody in particular, staring into space. 'I saw her ...' and she covered her face with her hands, remembering the horrible vision from the night before. The giggling and laughter stopped immediately, and everyone stared at her.

Turner went cold, the hairs on the back of his neck standing up. As calmly as he could he asked, 'What do you mean, Jade? Who is Kami? Who did you see.' He tried desperately to keep the quavering out of his voice.

She looked up slowly, her eyes moist. 'A young lady, Chinese or Japanese I couldn't tell, but ... she was cut ... everywhere ... and her face ... her face ...' and she thrust her head in her hands, sobbing loudly this time, her whole body convulsing and shaking in her grief. 'She talked to me ... she said ... she could see me ...'

Turner froze. This is what he had heard the hollow spectral voice say to him at Oswin Hall.

'Did she say her name was Kami?' he asked hesitatingly. The matter-of-fact way he was questioning her about this crazy story shocked Lee and Sandra, who were still trying to take in what the hell she was talking about.

'No,' Jade said, shaking her head. 'All she said was, she saw me and … then … started moving her arms towards me … I tried to escape. I must have fainted.' Jade was trembling uncontrollably, and Turner reached out and put his arm around her shoulder, slightly self-conscious about his lingering body odour.

'Kami isn't a name – it's our word for a spirit or a life force. It doesn't really translate very well into English. The nearest word I guess is "spirit" or "ghost" – though some people translate it as "God" as well - it's very confusing to Westerners.' She was trying to explain Eastern philosophy to a table full of people steeped in the traditions and beliefs of Western culture, and Lee had heard enough.

Deciding that Turner had brought yet another nut case home, he signalled the same to Sandra by pointing his finger at his head and turning it in rapid circles like an electric screwdriver, the mime for mental, pulling a funny face at the same time. Sandra suppressed a giggle, and thankfully Turner and Jade were too engrossed in each other to notice it.

Lee stood up, grabbing the dog's lead off the counter. 'Look, we'll take the dog out for his morning constitutionals while you guys talk psychic stuff, OK?' By psychic he really meant crazy, mad, loony tune crap but thought this sounded better. Sandra took the hint, and they made a quick exit.

Turner knew about Japanese Kami. He had to – as part of his work pretending to be a master psychic medium he was forced to learn about all superstitions and spiritual phenomena in cultures from around the world since ancient times. The bookcase in his bedroom was full of texts on all manner of beliefs and rituals, and he re-read them frequently to keep the knowledge fresh in his head. Throwing the odd bizarre fact into a reading or talk did wonders to convince his audience he truly was a master spiritualist. He had learnt long ago that if you say something confidently enough, even if it's a complete lie, then the general public tends to believe it. At the end of the day, politicians were using the same technique on a daily basis so why shouldn't he? A little knowledge could go a long way.

Kami, he'd read, was a spirit or life force trapped between our world and the spiritual plane. The Egyptians had called it a 'ka' or a 'khu' if the spirit entered the body of a living soul, man or beast, and then forced it to do things against their will. In Western culture, the phenomenon was most often linked with the works of the devil. Turner knew that during medieval times those thought to be possessed by or witness to the devil's spirits were ritually hanged, burnt or drowned. The myth and tales associated with these legends had allowed him many opportunities to scare the life out of his clients, and they'd paid him well for it.

'I think she's a type we call an Aragami, judging by the wounds on her body,' whispered Jade now they were alone. 'You know something too, don't you? Otherwise, you would have said I was crazy. I know you understand what I'm saying.' She looked up hopefully at him, her eyes pleading for the truth.

Turner did. He knew that in Japanese legend an Aragami was an avenging spirit that had been wronged in life, and had returned to wreak an often bloody and always fatal revenge on the wrongdoers. He'd found similar tales of avenging spirits described in terrible detail in the West. The French savant

Camille Flammarion told many such horrific tales in the third volume of *Death and its Mystery*, one of the books in Turner's prized esoteric book collection. Hence, he knew exactly what she meant, and it made him very uncomfortable.

How could all this be real? he thought, catching an accusing glimpse of his burnt cowboy boots in the corner of the kitchen. What had he done that had put an avenging spirit on his trail and why wasn't he dead already if it was after him? All he'd heard, or thought he'd heard, was a hollow voice. Plus, more importantly, he didn't believe in this stuff. The legends were tools of his trade, no more factual than a children's fairy tale. The whole story of the séance came spilling out of him to Jade. He found he couldn't hold back once he'd started. For the first time in his life, he was talking about spirit manifestations and was actually telling the truth. Turner the fake psychic medium was now becoming Turner the believer, and it absolutely terrified him to his soul.

CHAPTER 11

THE MASK SELLER

Jade studied the contents of the briefcase she'd tipped on the table the night before. Quickly spotting the orange brocade handkerchief wedged at the bottom of the pile, she grabbed it and looked up quizzically at Turner.

'Hey, what are you doing with this?' She was rubbing the thickly embroidered silk between her fingers.

'I found it under the seat of that French lady on the plane. I meant to give it back to her outside but she'd gone.' Turner felt like a petty thief but Jade could see by his expression that he was telling the truth.

'Well, you've just found the owner! It's mine – I've been looking for this everywhere. See how thick and well worked the cloth is? It was a gift from my parents – always reminds me of back home. Just tell me you haven't blown your nose on it?' she said, inspecting the cloth for any tell-tale marks before folding it and tucking it neatly inside her short kimono jacket.

'No, honest. I've taken good care of it,' replied Turner, omitting the fact he'd used it as a tablecloth under the carved box at the séance. The handkerchief must have fallen from her clothing when she had her jocular fit at his goldfish expression on the plane.

Satisfied, Jade picked up the carved box from the table and studied the designs beautifully engraved on it. 'You say you used this in the séance on Saturday?' Turner nodded.

'Somehow the spirit I saw must be tied to this box,' she said in a matter-of-fact way as if she was stating the obvious.

Carefully she examined the design, using her fingers to feel all around the curves of the deep carving. 'I'm not familiar with these shapes and patterns. Have you seen them before?'

Turner had, many times. 'It's very common here – used a lot in Scottish jewellery and that kind of thing. I think it's originally pagan, used by the old religions long before Christianity. I've never seen a box like this before though. The workmanship is incredible.'

As Jade tilted it back and forward to look at the various swirling patterns, it rattled loudly. Instinctively, she dropped it in fright. Nothing happened. She picked it up again and moved it from side to side, this time more vigorously. Something inside was following her movement and banging against the wood. Opening the lid, she could see the empty red silk- lined interior – there was no obvious source of the noise. Then she smiled to herself.

'Look – it's a puzzle box. How clever!' she explained delightedly. Jade showed Turner the very faint marks in the parquetry on the glossy base. The bottom of the box was not made from one piece of solid wood as it appeared, but many pieces of rectangular black ebony veneer. The black-on-black glossy lacquer made this almost impossible to spot. The thought of solving a puzzle seemed to have wiped away any fear from Jade, and she was positively excited.

As a youngster, she had played with many boxes similar to this, just as a Western child will spend hours trying to solve a Rubik's cube. Most boxes were smaller and had a marked pattern of dark and light wood so the various veneers were easy to spot. Moving the veneers in a particular order would open a secret part of the box or open a secret drawer. Turner was more than familiar with the concept of hidden compartments, as he'd concealed many items in a variety of cunning ways to create spooky effects in his psychic performances.

Without any hesitation, Jade started trying to crack the puzzle of the box. Turner was beginning to love this impulsive and wild side to her. She had a firm belief in getting on with things, living life and overcoming any problems she might face. It was infectious and soon he was offering suggestions on where to press or slide the veneers. They wouldn't move.

As if understanding something, Jade turned her attention to the red silk interior and began to slowly and very carefully poke and prod every minute part of the exposed lining with the point of her long fingernails. After a lengthy fifteen minutes, she finally felt a raised piece of wood under the lining. It was tiny, no bigger than a large pinhead. She pushed down hard on it, and a small piece of black veneer slid horizontally from the base. Removing it exposed another pinhead-sized piece of wood sticking out where the veneer had been. Again, she pushed hard and a second piece of veneer parallel to the first slid into her waiting hand. In total, there were five pieces like this that exposed an area of bare wood the size of a deck of playing cards on the base. Jade was delighted!

Now they were stuck again so she went back to feel inside the box. Sure enough, removing the five strips had raised another tiny area in a different part of the interior. Using the very tip of her manicured nail, she pressed down hard on it. A small wooden tray with raised sides crashed loudly onto the table, finally released from its locked hiding place in the bottom of the box. They both jumped again and Jade let out a little squeal of joy when she realised they'd done it.

Turner couldn't take his eyes off the pale wooden tray. There was a small-carved ivory figure, a pink slip of paper and what looked like a navy-blue bound booklet sitting in it. But it was the carved ivory figure that was holding his attention.

'At least that solves the mystery of the rattle,' he said, picking up the little figure. 'It must have been sliding around in its secret compartment as we moved the box around.'

Overall, the figure was no longer than his thumb and it looked very, very old. He moved it to the tips of his fingers, bringing it close to his face. There was a barely detectable whiff of decay as he turned it carefully, examining it from every angle.

It was a beautiful and incredibly detailed carving of an old man carrying a sack filled to the brim with masks. His back was bowed under the heavy load, giving him a hunchback appearance. Some of the masks had fallen and landed around the sandals on his feet. Turner guessed it was hewn from elephant ivory made in a time long before such practices were illegal. The quality of the work was absolutely staggering and incredibly lifelike. There was something about the face Jade recognised and, with a gasp, she realised the general structure and shape of it was identical to the spirit that had appeared to her. The carved masks held the same common features but each was distinctly different in some way. It was as if somebody had recreated the faces of their entire ancestral family within the diorama of the figure. Old wizened features mixed with smooth young complexions in the jumbled array of masks poking out of the figure's bulging sack. One mask at the hunched figure's feet was distinctly different and made from a deep amber material. Jade took it from him and peered at it closely. She shrieked in horror and dropped it on the table.

'That's her ... that's the grotesque face of the girl, the one from last night!' Jade was shaking again, reliving the memory in her head.

Turner picked it up like it was an unexploded bomb. The maimed amber features were contorted in agony, and the face littered with raised blemishes that looked like oozing sores. Channels cut to represent trickles of blood ran down from the hollow eye sockets. Jade turned a pallid grey, gripping the edge of the table to steady her hands. Turner got her a glass of water, and she sipped slowly as they sat in silence, staring at their find. Jade spotted some Japanese writing carved in green stone inlaid into its base.

'Kamo. The base says Kamo Clan in Japanese,' and without thinking she bowed her head in a reverential Japanese greeting to the prone figure lying upon the table. 'The Kamo Clan are a very ancient and well-respected samurai family in Japan,' she explained to Turner, slightly embarrassed at her involuntary nod when she read the name.

'This type of figure is called a netsuke, or katabori-netsuke to be exact. See the two holes in the base?' She leaned over to show him and he nodded. 'That's where a cord passed through. These carvings were basically ancient fasteners used to secure things to kimonos – kimonos don't have any storage pockets.'

Turner still looked confused so she decided to give him more background on the culture she knew so well: 'Japan's "Red and White Dragon War" in the twelfth century removed the last traces of our aristocracy. It put the warrior class, the White Dragons of the samurai, in charge. The samurai had many powerful families, similar to the clan structures in your Highlands of Scotland, and the Kamo Clan were one of the biggest and most revered, based around the ancient capital city of Kyoto.' Jade's mini history lesson was helping calm her nerves and Turner could understand the idea of powerful clans easily.

After another sip of water she continued, 'When the Dragon War finished many things changed. Women of a higher class were allowed to walk openly in the streets for the first time. Before that, they went everywhere in carriages carried by porters. It was a huge shift in our culture. To carry personal belongings like money, family seals or medicines they used a pouch or decorative box secured to their kimono by cords and a netsuke like this one. The netsuke were treasured possessions made by master carvers, passed from generation to generation and never sold outside of the family line. So the owner of this netsuke is from a very ancient and powerful Japanese bloodline.'

With new respect, Turner carefully stood the figure upright on the table as Jade went on with her tale. 'The carved box is very modern; the design is definitely not Japanese, must be made somewhere in the West.' Picking up the dismantled components, she wafted them under her nose. 'All I can smell is resin.' Reaching down she carefully picked up the ivory netsuke and repeated her smell test. 'There's something wrong here – there is a faint smell of decay, like food that's gone bad or something. I think the spirit of the girl is somehow stuck in the netsuke not the box. That would explain why she's Asian not Western looking.' She passed the box over, and he sniffed at it gingerly, fearing it might somehow slam shut and nip his nose. Turner felt foolish.

'This is stupid! What the hell are we doing sniffing things? I feel like I'm taking part in some perverted fetish movie, *Fifty Shades of Smell* or something!' he said, using gallows humour to mask his growing feeling of disquiet.

Jade didn't laugh. 'I'm telling you, Nathen that amber carving at the base of the netsuke is meant to be her. That's definitely the face of the spirit I saw last night.' He knew from her voice that she was deadly serious. His mind flicked back to the hollow voice and the roaring flames from the séance. How could he argue that something supernatural wasn't going on? He'd heard the spirit's voice, and evidence of his experience was staring back at him from his burnt footwear in the corner.

Frustrated and desperate to take his mind off the sense of foreboding creeping over him, he grabbed up the torn pink slip of paper from the hidden compartment. 'This looks like some form of council receipt. It's got the stamped oval logo for the borough of Scarborough, but I can't tell what it's for as the bottom's been ripped off.'

It certainly looked like a receipt. It was dated September 1994 in blue fountain pen at the very top, and the ink had bled through the thin paper to the other side. In a different hand to the date, someone had written on the back of the paper in black biro:

Kat,
See you tonight after the show – usual place!
Love you lots.

There were some initials as well but the blue fountain-pen ink that had bled through the paper made them illegible. All that was visible were the outlines of several kisses and a badly drawn heart.

Jade was ignoring him and loudly tapping the upside-down wooden compartment onto the table top in an attempt to release the little blue booklet that was wedged at the bottom, her curiosity now on full beam.

After more brutal tapping, the rectangular booklet sprung loose and flew across the table. She stretched over to get it and Turner grabbed her hand. 'Do we really want to do this? Can't we just put everything back and return the box to Oswin Hall? I'm scared, Jade … really scared.' Facing the fact that there was a real spirit realm and not just a fake one he created for unwitting clients was terrifying him. What if the spirits had been watching him con all those decent people? A decade of deceit lay heavy on his conscience and, for the first time in his life, he felt ashamed of what he'd done.

Jade quickly reached over with her free hand and deftly flicked open the book, ignoring his plea. There she was, or more accurately what she used to be. The facial shape and general features were unmistakably that of the ghoulish girl who appeared in the kitchen, but the passport-sized photograph showed her smiling gaily into the lens without a care in the world. Her makeup was styled as a goth, with heavy black eyeliner and dark lipstick on a pale complexion. A long black fringe formed a straight line across her forehead just above her eyebrows, with long side strands covering her ears and cascading over her shoulders. The photograph was held in place by yellowing and peeling Sellotape, and above it were stamped the words 'KATSUMI KAMO' and slightly below '09 06 76' in hard black type. The rest of that page had her signature and some small print certifying her as a registered student of Leeds University and the student union. Recognising the unmarked and innocent face in the smiling photograph upset Jade and she began to cry.

'It's her student card. Look at her – she's so beautiful and seems so happy,' she said, quietly sobbing sadly, tears dripping down onto the floor.

Flicking through the rest of the stapled pages, they found her address in Leeds as 'Room 265, Mary Ogilvie House, Charles Morris Hall' and a green worded sticker had been applied on the previous page simply stating, 'CHARLES MORRIS HALL 1994–95'. Turner figured this had to be the same goth student Juliet Armstrong had told Lee about – the one who'd left the hotel without a forwarding address.

Now he was on a mission. Frantically scanning through the small booklet, he let out a whoop of sheer joy. 'I've found it! We've got her Japanese home address here as well. All we have to do is put the box back together and post it back to her!'

Jade stared at him like he'd gone completely mad. Turner froze in the icy glare, wondering what was wrong with his idea. From his point of view, they couldn't get rid of their find quick enough. The sooner he could forget about it the better and then with time pretend it never happened.

'You know she's dead, right? You know she has to be? This girl in the photograph – Katsumi Kamo – she is the spirit that appeared to me; that's what's left of her now. The shape of the face is exactly the same. I'm positive it's her.' Turner picked up the ivory figure and studied the features on the amber mask, comparing it with the photograph. All he kept saying was, 'Oh my God, Oh my God ...' over and over again as his gaze passed repeatedly between the two.

Jade watched the realisation dawn on Turner, saw the fear on his face. 'Now you see, don't you? It's definitely her. These Kami, these ghosts or spirits as you call them, are the life force of the dead, not some psychic messaging service for the living. Somehow her troubled spirit has bound itself to this netsuke. If she were alive, we would never have seen or heard her ghost. And I've told you about the scars and cuts on her body. She's dead, Nathen, very dead, and for some reason, she's after us.'

All the years of deception were now literally coming back to haunt Nathen Turner.

CHAPTER 12

SMOKE AND PANDAS

'Why can't he ever find a normal, sane person?' Lee Melone complained to Sandra Vaughan walking at his side. The dog by now was bounding ahead, enjoying the crispness of the late-morning air and the feel of the cobblestones under his big shaggy paws.

'The last one was a tripped-out hippy; the one before that was convinced she was a reincarnation of Marilyn Monroe. This one sees dead bodies in our kitchen! I mean, what the hell! Is it me, or is he just attracted to bloody bunny boilers?' Sandra was laughing at the rant, then pulled up short.

Gazing ahead she could see a line of police cars blocking the road past St. Hilda's Church and on into Victoria Square. The entire area was full of bustling uniformed police officers looking very stern as they held back the curious crowd. Their fluorescent overcoats were reflecting the flashing lights from the top of the stationary panda cars, causing a weird rippling light show. They kept walking, following the road as it bent round to the right, past the church, and found wavy lines of blue and white 'DO NOT CROSS' police tape restricting access to the junction and the entrance to Oswin Hall Hotel. Lee spotted a familiar face pulling heavily on a cigarette just outside the door of the hotel.

'Joe, Joe!' he shouted, waving both hands above his head like a swimmer trying to call for help. Detective Inspector Joe

Stewart turned to find the source of the noise, irritated that his nicotine fix had been interrupted. He spotted Lee in the crowd and shouted to one of the uniformed officers to let him through. Leaving Sandra and the dog behind, Lee ducked under the tape and jogged over to the inspector, getting a face full of second-hand smoke for his trouble.

Stewart looked tired. He'd been awake all night cleaning up a horrific and bloody traffic accident caused by a reckless drunk driver before getting a call to come straight to Oswin Hall. In his work he'd seen so much death and violence that it had ceased to bother him. Now he pushed through one crime scene after another like an emotionless automaton. Only after a few drinks did the outer hard façade fall and he would weep into the night until his alcohol-doused brain lapsed into unconsciousness. His three-piece tweed suit was dirty and wrinkled, and he'd pulled off his tie some time ago.

Stewart had been the first police officer on the scene when Tony, Lee's Hep Cats drummer, had taken his car over the top of Flamborough Head, high on drugs. Since then they'd see each other now and again around the town and always have a catch-up on the local gossip and the latest minor miracle Turner had pulled off. In truth, Stewart had developed an interest in the occult and supernatural as a child, spawned from watching Hammer Horror movies with his family in their remote cottage in the Highlands of Scotland. *Friday Fright Night* on the BBC had become a major attraction in their house, watched with the lights off and the sound turned up. That was the era when horror movies actually had a plot and weren't just sensationalised gore fests to demonstrate how good the special effects team were. He'd developed a geek interest in all supernatural creatures and avidly munched his way through scores of packets of crisps to collect enough tokens to send off for a range of monster medallions that Tudor Crisps were offering. The Werewolf, the Sphinx, and the Gorgon's Head: he loved them all and would eagerly show off his latest metal monster pendants to his friends at school. While they were playing with Action Man, he was painting the latest Dracula glow-in-the-dark plastic model kit. The fascination never left him, and finally he moved south to Whitby thirty-odd years ago specifically to be around the birthplace of the Dracula legend. He adored the annual goth festival and had been on duty at every one since they started. Seeing the incredible black costumes and fanciful makeup reminded him of the best parts of his childhood – the times when it was OK to dream, to fantasise without being judged. The festivals had also provided more than he could have imagined when he met his wife at one of the early events. After arresting her for being drunk and disorderly, he'd given her a caution and his phone number. Now they were settled and happy with two small children, living in an apartment overlooking Whitby Abbey and its grounds.

'Well, hello there, Hurricane! That's a bonny lass you're with today,' he said, pointing at the dog. 'And the girl's OK as well,' he continued, laying on a thick Scottish accent. He'd lost most of his Highland brogue years ago when he moved south but always put it on thick if he was joking with Lee. Stewart was using Lee's affectionate nickname of 'Guitar Hurricane' from his time in the Hep Cats.

'Thought you'd quit,' Lee said, laughing and nodding at the smouldering cigarette wedged in the corner of his mouth.

'Bollocks to that doing this job! Those electronic cigs are like puffing on stale air with pig sweat in. Give me the good old cancer fix any day,' he countered, his regular southern-based accent returning. 'I did quit one whole day though – then was up for seventy-two hours on a robbery case. So it was welcome back, Mr Nicotine,' he said, flicking the smoking butt onto the floor and grinding it out with his foot. Lee noticed another eight or ten already there so he must have been outside for a while. Stewart saw Lee glancing down at the pile of tobacco debris: 'Scene-of-crime boys are in – been stuck outside for two hours,' he explained without being asked. He was a great detective and observing others' behaviour and reading it was certainly one of his major strong points.

As if on cue, a huge figure in a white paper boiler suit, white paper overshoes and white mask opened the side door of the hotel and walked down the short stone path to Stewart and Lee.

'Who's he?' said the tall white figure gruffly, removing the mask to reveal a neatly trimmed dark beard.

'He's OK, Paul. He's helping me with enquiries,' he said, winking slightly in Lee's direction so that the bearded giant couldn't see.

'Well, it's a strange one, I must say, guv,' he said more softly, removing his white hood and running his hand through his neat centre-parted black hair. 'Looks like suicide to me but not like your regular run of the mill ones – there's a few complications.'

He went on to explain that the cause of death according to the coroner was asphyxiation by hanging – which made perfect sense as the body was found hanging from the upstairs balcony with a rope noose around their neck. But most depressive suicide types used simple securing knots and slipknots, and washing line cord or similar, to do the deed. This noose had been professionally tied with a knot known as a 'Duncan's Loop' normally used by fishermen to attach hooks, rings or swivels to the end of their line. Also, the rope was the thick orange type very common in the harbour for attaching baited fishing traps to marker buoys. They'd looked around and couldn't find any other supplies of that type in the building but there was plenty of washing line and similar strong cord.

'The other weird thing is that the little finger on the left hand was broken in two places. It must have been really painful but there is no sign of any bandaging to protect it or any obvious cause for the injury. Here is the note – we've dusted it but leave it in the bag, will you?' Paul handed him a transparent police evidence bag with a small piece of paper inside. 'Anyway, got to go and write all this up,' he said, and with that he stomped off purposefully to a waiting police car.

Stewart turned the bagged suicide note in his hands and looked at the untidy handwriting in the scrawled blue fountain pen visible through the transparent sides. The scene-of-crime officer was right – there were some strange things here. When the cleaner had opened up that morning, she'd found the body hanging stiff and cold from a rope tied to the upstairs banister. The note was on a side table to the right of the hanging corpse. But there was no pen. Why would somebody not long for this world write a note then hide the pen? Also, the note was definitely written at that side table as some of the blue ink had gone through the paper and stained the woodwork below. And why was one of the stools in the main bar area in the other room standing on the floor when all the others were upside down on the top of the bar? Little things like this bothered him, and Lee could see he'd got lost in deep thought, turning things over and over in his mind.

'Suicide? Who on earth has committed suicide?' asked Lee quickly, shocked by what he'd just heard.

'Oh, didn't I say?' Stewart said, breaking off his train of thought. 'The owner, Juliet Armstrong. Don't think she could cope with the recent loss of her husband.'

CHAPTER 13

UNWELCOME VISITORS

The two hunched figures of Turner and Jade sat silently over the kitchen table, trying to make sense of what they'd discovered in the hidden compartment of the carved black box. Jade began carefully putting the parquetry veneer back together, minus its secret contents. The ivory carving, the slip of pink paper and worn blue student union booklet had been placed spaced out in a line on the kitchen table.

Turner busied himself at the kettle, using the mundane task of tea making again to take his mind off the horror and fear he felt. He smiled silently to himself, thinking that finally he understood the logic and beauty behind the Japanese tea ceremony. Back in ancient times, the tea ceremony represented peace and tranquillity amidst the violence of feudal Japan. Samurai warriors were not allowed to wear their swords at the ceremony, and any talk of politics or war was strictly forbidden. Suddenly, the whole thing made perfect sense to him.

A loud banging at the door broke his train of thought. Outside in the street were two huge men. One was in a red checked wool work shirt with sleeves rolled up to the elbows and the other in a black leather jacket and black polo shirt. Both wore black jeans, and polished heavy steel-toe-capped boots. They looked like they'd been up all night. He opened the door and thought he caught a brief whiff of stale fish and salt, assuming the tide must be out and the drying seaweed was letting its presence be known.

'You Turner, Nathen Turner, the psychic medium guy?' asked red-checked shirt man gruffly holding, up one of Turner's white business cards and exposing the naval tattoo on his muscular forearm. Turner had two different business cards. One was a colourful double-sided affair stating his name, an email address and phone number only. It was decorated with swirling blue and purple clouds and the phrase 'Confidential Psychic Medium' under his name. The second was the card he reserved for past clients only. It was a plain white card with his name, address and a different mobile number and email address. The method had worked well as he could keep most of the loonies at bay using the first card, blocking their calls or emails if he needed to. The white card made his past clients feel exclusive and brought him more trade as they could now write to him for advice or call him on his special private line. They paid a premium rate for this privilege of course. The two bears dressed as people standing before him were certainly not past clients of his.

'Where'd you get that card?' Turner asked as sternly as he could but feeling intimidated by the giant men.

'From a mutual friend of ours, Juliet Armstrong, over at the Hotel,' check shirt said, gesturing vaguely in the direction of Oswin Hall across the river. 'She told us you've got something that belongs to us – a carved black box she'd given you by mistake the other night. You see, we gave it to her husband for safekeeping. I suppose she wasn't to know, so no harm done, eh? We want it back.' It wasn't a question. It was a direct order, and the guy in the black jacket took a half pace forward towards Turner, his eyes boring into him, challenging him to refuse.

Turner knew this was a total lie. The box belonged to the student Katsumi Kamo; they'd proved that from the contents of the hidden compartment. How could it possibly belong to these two thugs?

It was the best cover story Roby had come up with, and he wasn't expecting any trouble from a crackpot idiot who thought he was in touch with the supernatural.

'Have you still got the box?' Roby demanded, stepping closer. Turner could smell his pungent breath reeking of stale beer from the night before.

Turner turned his face slightly to the side for cleaner air. 'I have no idea what you are talking about. Let me call Juliet; I'm sure we can sort this out.' He reached down for the kitchen door handle and Pearson grabbed his wrist in a vice-like grip.

'There's no need for that, is there, between friends like us?' he whispered menacingly in his ear. The smell of fish on him was unmistakable and Turner involuntarily recoiled from it. Pearson followed his movement and gripped harder. 'There, there. No need to run away, my friend. Let's have a nice cosy chat, shall we?' he hissed.

'Lee, Lee! Hi, man. Had a good walk?' Lee Melone had appeared at the end of the street with Sandra at his side and Kyle pulling him like he was in charge of a dog-sled team. Turner had never been so pleased to see his friend in his life, and he positively beamed at him. Lee was too far away to hear him so Turner used his free hand to wave, and Lee waved back, wondering why he was up close and personal with two gigantic men. Was he finally turning to the pink side now, as well as regularly bringing home nut cases? Live and let live, he thought, and kept walking.

Kyle got to the doorway first and started barking loudly at the two strangers, sensing something was wrong. Pearson lost his grip and took a step back. 'These guys have a message from Juliet Armstrong,' Turner explained, nodding at the two brooding chaps.

'Not again – are these bloody psychic weirdos as well?' Lee said, opening his arms in a gesture of sheer exasperation. Turner was confused.

'What do you mean, psychic? She's just a hotel owner not a medium,' he tried to explain.

'Yes, a very dead hotel owner. She committed suicide this morning. So unless these boys have a Batphone to heaven then they must be bloody psychic, right?' Lee said flatly as if it was obvious.

Roby and Pearson looked at Lee with a cold dead stare, then at each other and nodded. 'That's terrible news – and she was so full of life.' Lee could swear he could see the one in the black jacket smirking to himself as his companion said this. 'We'll continue our chat another time, Mr Turner; you've no idea how much we are looking forward to seeing you again.' And with that they turned and walked calmly away towards the harbour.

'What the hell was all that about? Who were they – King Kong's lost love children?' Lee asked, staring after them.

'I don't know,' Turner said, sniggering at Lee's remark about the two goons. 'Did you say suicide? She seemed in pretty good shape last time I saw her. Come in – Jade's found something you should see.'

'Bloody great – can't wait,' said Lee desperately trying to figure out where else he could go to get away from this ridiculous talk. Kyle pulled him into the kitchen, making a mad dash for his water bowl. Lee just had time to smile meekly at Jade sitting down at the table as the dog yanked him forward and sent him skidding to the other side of the room. For the next hour he sat patiently listening to the tale of their discovery while Sandra paced impatiently up and down behind him.

'Right, that's it. I've heard enough!' Sandra said, moving to the bottom of the stairs. 'Enough is enough. I've got to let off some steam before I hit some bugger.' Her Australian accent came through loud and clear in her frustration. 'Look, Lee, I'm sorry but I can't take any more of this. I'll see you upstairs. All sounds way too crazy to me. Just give the box and all the other crap over to the police and have done with it.' With that, Sandra skulked off muttering 'nutter,' 'idiot' and a lot of other phrases that really did not befit a lady.

'I need a drink.' Lee followed her and ten minutes later was snuggled up in his favourite lounge armchair, puffing on a fat cigar.

The cigar smoke billowed from the open lounge window as Lee sat back contemplating life, the universe and the fine tobacco glowing in his hand. He found cigars helped him relax – the entire ritual of lighting one slowed him right down and he loved the soft velvet feel of the outer leaf as he rolled it sensuously between his fingers. From his touring days, he'd found that puffing away slowly and talking into the night about music and women had proved a fantastic way to unwind after the adrenalin high of performance. The box of cigars Turner had brought him back from Las Vegas lay open on the table to his right, together with a tray of long cigar matches, a half empty tumbler of whisky and a huge and heavy glass ashtray.

Lee's attention was being continually distracted to his left by the bouncing Lycra-clad behind of Sandra, sweating and moving to some American fitness DVD. She was taking out her frustration by punching the air and kicking in time to the figures on the screen. Scattered at her feet were another half dozen DVD cases with colourful titles like *Buns of Steel*, *Awesome Abs* and *Fight the Flab in only 5 minutes a day!* The one she appeared to be working out to now was a weird combination of kick boxing and yoga and he certainly was enjoying the view. He hated the hip-hop music but it was a price worth paying to watch her seductive body lithely leaping across the room. Lee idly wondered if they'd ever do one with a blues music backing-track called something like *Depress Yourself Fit* and he chuckled to himself at the thought.

He could hear Jade on the phone downstairs, talking in tense Japanese. Listening to her excited and sometimes raised tones made him think they were having some sort of an argument back and forth. As this war of words took place in the background, Turner had joined him upstairs, trying to explain again in a trembling voice about the netsuke figure and the spooky visit of Katsumi Kamo's ghost. When he got to the point of describing the latter as some form of dead spirit with dripping blood and hollow black eyes, Lee downed his tumbler of whisky in one, then poured another. Lee had seen all Turner's tricks before and neither he, nor Sandra, bought into the story. They were telling him so when Jade joined them with a bunch of scribbled notes written in spidery kanji characters.

She looked stressed and agitated, constantly tapping her fingers on the parcel of thin paper.

'I've spoken to my grandmother and told her everything.' This confirmed as far as Lee was concerned that Jade's entire family were obviously bonkers. 'She has ordered me to leave and head back to London right now – but I've refused.' Turner reached over and covered her hand to stop her fingers tapping, in a gentle gesture meant to calm her a little. She pulled away, determined to finish what she was saying. 'We have argued ... a lot ... and she is very unhappy with me. But if I feel I must stay, she says we must surround the netsuke with a ring of salt. The spirits cannot pass the purity of the salt barrier.'

'We haven't got any salt, and the spirits are passing my barrier just fine,' Lee slurred bluntly and took another slug of whisky.

Ignoring him, Jade continued, 'My grandmother says we must find out what the spirit wants and, if it is within our power, give it to them. Otherwise, the spirit can never be at peace – something is still holding her soul to the mortal world, and she's trapped in what you Westerners call 'limbo'. She thinks it's not after us, or we'd be dead by now.'

'Thinks? Oh, that's really reassuring, that is. You've got to be joking, right? This is a major wind-up. Nathen, come on, own up! Where's the cameras?' Lee drained his glass again and grinned stupidly around the room, playing to the hidden cameras he assumed were there.

Jade and Turner just looked at him and said nothing. Their expressions said it all to Lee – whatever he thought, both of them definitely believed this spiritual nonsense.

'How do we find out what she wants?' Turner asked quietly, almost to himself.

'There is a ceremony from one of the old kaidan tales my grandmother heard as a child that she says should work. These stories are like your folk tales and one of them is a very famous story of a restless spirit. It talks about a ritual to call out the ghost of a dead man ...' She stopped abruptly.

'What? Go on ...' Lee was now impatient to see this madness to its conclusion.

'Well, in this particular tale the ritual goes to plan but ...' Jade looked around at all of them sheepishly. 'Erm ... well ... then things go a bit wrong, and everybody dies – the spirit kills them all.'

'Terrific, just bloody terrific.' Lee grabbed the half empty whisky bottle and downed it in one.

CHAPTER 14

DANGER AT SEA

The early morning newspaper stands were dramatically proclaiming, 'Horror at the Hall – Read all about it' and their trade was booming. In the town the news had been received the same way people around the world handle tragic news stories when they have no real emotional attachment to those involved. After the first morning reports had been and gone, the locals muttered sympathetically about how sad it all was and then moved on with their lives.

After visiting Turner, Roby and Pearson had set sail on the morning's high tide, heading for their crab and lobster pots six miles out from the harbour mouth. Pearson expertly manoeuvred the small fishing boat close to his red marker buoy bobbing gently in the swell. The journey had not been smooth as they were heading wind against tide and the breaking waves had frequently flooded the small flat deck. Now the wind was dropping, making it easy for Roby to hook the buoy line and feed it into the electric winch. Neither man spoke. The sea was their home, and they had done this so often that both men knew exactly what the other one had to do.

Reaching over the side with his thick blue rubber gloves, Roby grabbed the first dripping pot as it came galloping out of the water. He expertly spun it onto the side rail of the boat and unclipped the small mesh door. Thick orange nylon netting cocooned the semi-circular pot, and he gingerly lifted out a mottled dark greenish-brown lobster, waving it triumphantly in the air. Pearson gave a thumbs-up from the small wheelhouse just before the next pot came crashing in. Quickly re-baiting the first pot, he stacked it on the deck and grabbed the second. Fishing had generally been poor; dredging had seen to that. It was a constant battle to find lucrative grounds that hadn't been destroyed by the aggressive scraping of the seabed. The locals were up in arms but the politicians as usual were turning a blind eye to Whitby's declining commercial fishing industry. Promoting tourism and leisure fishing got them more votes and TV time.

On they went with the steady routine – haul, empty, re-bait, stack – until nine pots were piled neatly at the rear of the slippery wooden deck. Nothing else had found its way through any of the pots' one-way funnels, and the solitary lobster twitching in the plastic bucket at Roby's feet was all they had to show for their efforts. Selling it wouldn't even cover the cost of the diesel to get to the fishing grounds. Neither of the men worried about this today. It wasn't the fishing they had come for.

The last pot clunked heavily against the side of the boat and Roby was really struggling to lift it on board. He placed it straight down on the deck, a grim smile on his face. The mesh access door ran the entire length of the pot and was secured by two thick bungee cords and moulded plastic clips. Kneeling, he unhooked the overly large panel and slowly pulled out a military-grade plastic yellow suitcase. It was tough-going as the corners snagged and pulled at the orange netting, causing a torrent of swearing over the clatter of the boat's engine. Finally, it slithered out, covered in sand and seaweed from its time on the ocean floor. He refastened the empty pot and stacked it with the others.

The boat turned slowly, heading south against the swell, and motored for another fifteen minutes before they threw the newly baited pots back into their watery home. Pearson cut the engine and joined Roby on deck. Carefully he turned the knurled black plastic knob that sat centrally on the top of the case. Air rushed out, blowing dregs of sand and seaweed across the dirty yellow surface. With the air pressure now equalised inside and out, they cleaned up the combination lock and opened it. Inside were six ballistic syringes, about the shape and size of a silver fountain pen, with fibrous red tailpieces. Etched on each steel cylinder was 'WARNING – M99. Licensed veterinary use only' next to a black outline of a small skull and crossbones. Above the cylinders in a custom-cut foam interior were two black dart guns of a similar shape and size to those used in paintball skirmishes. More plain steel cylinders were stacked either side. These were completely different and looked more like sealed mini thermos flasks. Roby picked one of them up and screwed it carefully into the skeleton handgrip on one of the guns. There was a brief hiss as the carbon dioxide gas it contained leaked out before the seal was fully made. He pointed the empty gun at the rear of the boat and pulled the trigger. 'PFFT!' A quick and loud release of gas confirmed the air weapon was now primed and ready for use. After testing both guns the same way, he sat back, very pleased with himself.

'These will sort that bloody dog if we get any trouble. Them too. If we have to,' Roby said, breaking the silence and casually stroking a gun barrel. He knew the tranquilliser M99, or etorphine hydrochloride as it was properly known, could immobilise an elephant. He got up and scanned the radio frequencies in the wheelhouse to see if there had been any further developments on the Juliet Armstrong death. Nothing. As far as he could see, they were in the clear. Heading offshore had been a double benefit as it also potentially gave them an alibi if no one looked too close at the timings. He was pretty sure their 'friend' in the police force could help with that.

They needed friends in high places. As the fishing had slowly dried up, Pearson had turned to smuggling as his main source of income. His old friend Roby was the perfect accomplice as the harbour watchkeeper. All they had to do was drop empty crab pots in a designated location, wait twenty-four hours, then retrieve them. In the meantime, small craft, mainly from Holland, would pick them up overnight, fill them with contraband and drop them back again. All the smuggled goods were packed carefully in watertight ex-military cases of varying shapes, colours and sizes to fit the pots. Using this method they'd been able to bring in mobile phones, drugs, alcohol and cigarettes and even handle the odd special request from their clientele. Once a month the empty military cases would be picked up on the end of a weighted buoy line and recycled for the next drop. When the dart gun had appeared, they didn't know what to do with it. Bringing it on land would be a major and unnecessary risk. UK firearms law was incredibly strict and if they got caught with it, they'd face a hefty prison sentence. So it stayed in the ocean ready for that special occasion. Well, today was the day – they had a dog and a crazy psychic to intimidate.

Pearson restarted the engine and turned the boat back

towards shore. They spotted the cardinal buoy guarding the eastern rocky shoreline one mile north of the harbour and pushed the nose of the boat into the growing swell. Sea spray jetted up and across the deck, causing Roby to pull his yellow oilskins tighter around him. He called up bridge control on the radio and asked them to be ready to open the swing bridge to give access to the marina. The boat puttered in past the tall stone harbour walls and along to their mooring. With the dart guns and spare ammunition safely stashed in an innocent-looking rucksack, the two sailors hopped ashore and grabbed a seat in the nearest café. They needed to be seen returning from sea. Pearson had brought the writhing lobster along in the bucket and offered to trade it for two frothy coffees and a couple of fry-ups. Sheila Preston, the buxom owner of Carlo's Café, eagerly agreed and disappeared into the kitchen.

Carlo's was much like every other seaside café up and down the east coast. The walls had originally been white but now were a mix of nicotine brown and dull cream. Scattered furniture littered the interior. It was probably trendy back in the sixties, but now it was just tired and wobbly. Grease stained the tables, and ketchup streaks crawled across the lower walls. The whole place smelt damp and musky. Local radio was playing a variety of out-of-date tunes with a tired DJ attempting vainly to make it interesting.

'Shocking about that suicide innit?' Sheila said dumping two huge plates of greasy food on the table. Fried eggs slid around madly on the cracked porcelain, saving themselves by diving between the burnt bacon and coagulated beans.

'What suicide? We've just got back in port. What happened?' Roby stuck half a rasher of crispy bacon in his mouth, relishing the smoky taste.

'That whatshername from the Hall. You know, the snooty one that owns it. She's only gone an' hanged herself. Her husband died last week, you know. Poor cow couldn't face things without him.'

'I know how she feels. When my wife died, I felt like the world had ended. At least she's at peace now.' Roby was trying his best to sound sad and sympathetic.

'Amen to that,' she said, and bustled off to get the coffee.

'We're in the clear. I'm sure of it, Robbo.' Spatters of baked bean stuck on Pearson's stubbly chin giving him the look of a piratical hobo.

'You forget, we're not done yet. We've still got some business with that sodding psychic guy,' said Roby, waving his fork in the general direction of Turner's house. 'I bet his bloody fortune telling hasn't told him we're coming back!'

Laughing loudly at his own joke, Roby patted the rucksack with the dart guns and winked.

CHAPTER 15

MIRROR ON THE SOUL

Just as Roby and Pearson were hauling in their pots, Jade and Turner were shopping, feeling relieved to be out in the crisp clean air again. The items on her grandmother's list were eclectic to say the least. They were determined to carry out the ceremony from the folk tale, feeling it was as much for their own protection as well as to do with helping the tortured spirit of Katsumi Kamo. The irony of the situation was not lost on Turner. For most of his adult life, he'd been making a living faking these kinds of things. Now it was for real, he found the list of items even more bizarre than even he would have conjured up. Walking around he felt nervous and uneasy and still couldn't shake the feeling that something, or someone, was watching him everywhere he went.

From market place to pound shop, they scoured the town for three hours before they were finally done. The light was fading fast over the harbour when they returned, carrying their booty in three large bags. Kyle had greeted them warmly at the door, licking Jade's hand affectionately as before. Judging by the loud moaning and rhythmic grunting coming downstairs from Lee's room, he and Sandra had moved from aerobics to another form of exercise that involved both of them.

Turner left Jade to unpack while he took a shower and got changed into clean clothes. She was glad of the time on her own to reflect on the whirlwind of the last forty-eight hours.

Jade's wild side loved the roller-coaster ride it had been so far, but she couldn't shake the sense of foreboding hanging over the house. As she headed upstairs to freshen up, the loud erotic moaning from the other side of Lee's bedroom door made her stop in her tracks. There was no way she could get to her small bag of clothes with the two lovers occupying her temporary bedroom. On a whim, she headed upstairs to Turner's room and searched through his closet for anything she could change into. Her drive for cleanliness overcame any concerns about raiding his clothing supply, and she didn't think he'd mind anyway. Turner's vast array of Hawaiian shirts were as unisex as she could find so she chose a green one with a small white and yellow flower print. Digging through his drawers, she found the largest variety of concho belts she'd ever seen. Picking up a brown leather one with silver oval decorations, she secured it neatly around her slim waist, twisting the excess leather strap behind the main belt so it didn't hang down. Turner was a tall guy so fortunately for her the shirt reached to just about mid thigh on her diminutive five foot four inch frame. Not perfect but still respectable, she thought, gazing in his full-length mirror.

Turner walked into his bedroom to find this vision of Jade twisting and turning in front of his mirror. 'No – your bum doesn't look big in that!' he joked from across the room.

'You look pretty big in that,' she flirted right back, covering her surprise at his sudden appearance. He was naked except for a wet towel wrapped around his waist, and the brushed green cotton fabric was starting to bulge suspiciously outwards in an area directly between his legs. Looking down, his dripping hair causing pools of water to form on the carpet,

Turner immediately went red from embarrassment. She stalked seductively past him and kissed him lightly on the cheek. 'I'll leave you to get ready,' she whispered sensually into his ear, and left the room with a little cheeky pat on his covered behind.

Turner pulled on a very loud red shirt with yellow, green and white shrubs bursting out all over it. Smart boot-cut denim jeans and a large brass decorated belt completed the look. The red colour always lifted his spirits a little and he felt clean and refreshed as he headed downstairs.

Lee and Sandra had joined Jade in the lounge, looking a little sweaty but very relaxed. If anything, Lee looked more subdued than normal, probably down to the quantity of whisky he'd drunk in the afternoon. They watched in fascination as she laid out the produce from the shopping trip on the coffee table.

'We need to be near the fireplace as well so we'll have to do it over there,' said Jade pointing at the open fireplace and its oak surround that sat in the middle of the wall opposite the main settee.

She carefully placed the rectangular coffee table parallel to the fire, with its short sides facing the window and door respectively. Four chairs from the kitchen surrounded the table, two on each long side. Turner saw that Lee and Sandra had resolved to take part, although they kept nudging each other and raising their eyebrows in disbelief as Jade arranged the bizarre scene. The ivory carved figure of the mask seller was placed in the centre of the table, facing towards the window. Surrounding it, in a perfect white circle, was a large heaped mound of coarse sea salt, its crystal flakes shimmering in the light of the room. A broad white church candle marked each extreme corner of the wooden surface. Directly in front of the mask-seller figure, but outside the salt circle, an ornate mirror had been propped on its end. It was an old Victorian dressing mirror they'd found in the market, held steady and upright by a thick brass plate stand.

'When the spirit arrives, you must not look at it directly. You must look into the mirror only. Do not let your attention be distracted by anything else or we will all be in real danger,' Jade said matter-of-factly as she worked. Things had gone too far to question her now; this was her show, for better or worse. 'The mirror acts as our view into her world – into her soul, if you like,' she said, shivering slightly. Turner was pale and silent, standing near the door as if he wanted to run away. He had never done this for real and the prospect of doing so unnerved him. Slowly, as though being dragged to his doom, he walked to the table and sat down heavily.

Jade reached under the table and lifted a large transparent bowl of water from the floor, being extremely careful not to spill any. Sliding it gently between the figure and the mirror, she took her time making minor adjustments until she was happy with the alignment. Finally, from the last carrier bag she spilled out another large cylindrical white church candle, short knife, small white ceramic cake bowl and kitchen tongs. Carefully scraping the knife over the surface of the candle, she peeled thin strips of the shimmering wax into the bowl until it was overflowing with the greasy material. The clammy sweat on her brow and trembling hands gave away how much effort this was for her, even though she was trying to appear in complete control. Finally, she flicked through the notes from the phone call and then nodded. 'OK we're ready to go.'

'Where's the dog?' asked Turner quickly, worried he might come in and crash through all the careful preparation.

'I've shut him downstairs with some doggy treats and told him he has to guard the front door, so he's fine. He won't hear us up here with the doors shut,' Lee explained, and Turner relaxed and thanked him. While going through things in his mind he looked around the room, the fireplace reminding him of the first night he'd heard the hollow voice with Juliet Armstrong in the maisonette. Now she was dead and he was in his lounge, trying to summon a real supernatural being. He hung his head, ashamed of the bogus show he'd used to exploit Juliet's grief.

Jade noticed the gesture. Assuming he was worried about what was to come, her soft hands reached out and squeezed his forearm gently. He looked up at her beautiful green eyes and for the first time realised he was falling in love with this wild Asian bombshell. She could have left this madness far behind but instead had faced her fears and stayed.

'Are you ready?' Jade asked him softly so the others couldn't hear. He just nodded sullenly in reply and glanced over to see Lee and Sandra tightly holding hands and staring fixedly at the mirror. Jade lit the four corner candles with one of Lee's long cigar matches and then switched off the room lights. The gentle flickering illumination from the flames blended with the moonlight streaming through the window, creating a sea of soft moving shadows across the little ivory carving. It almost looked like it was breathing.

'Remember,' whispered Jade, 'whatever happens, just look in the mirror.'

The silence in the room was like a thick fog filled with fear and apprehension. Slowly, Jade began to chant smoothly in Japanese, the hypnotic phrasing amplifying the tension they all felt.

'*Watashi wa anata ni yobu watashi no senzo no rei,*' she recited from the slip of paper in her hand, calling on the spirit of her ancestors for help. '*Watashi no tangan o kiki, watashi ni kuru.*' On it went, over and over, the same two phrases filling the room, their gentle repeated rhythm helping to calm her quavering voice.

Then the fire behind the table burst into flames. It roared and leapt and spat upwards as if fuelled by some ungodly power. Lee and Sandra's cynicism vanished in the blaze and they gripped each other tightly, their gaze locked on the mirror. The smell of rotting flesh filled the room, the stench of decay flooding out from the direction of the netsuke.

Jade deftly grabbed the white ceramic bowl with the tongs and held it in the middle of the inferno raging in the hearth. The wax from the church candle instantaneously melted, and she quickly poured the oily white liquid into the centre of the large bowl of water in front of the mirror. The wax streamed into the cold water like fluffy white clouds billowing and blowing across the heavens.

'*Katsumi Kamo watashi wa watashi ni anata o yobidasu,*' she commanded loudly to the room. Nothing happened so she said it again more forcefully, ordering Katsumi Kamo's spirit to them.

The wax began to move through the water. Slowly it formed the shape of the contorted death mask of Katsumi Kamo they'd seen at the foot of the mask-seller netsuke. The amber-coloured mask on the ivory statue was melting into the carving and re-forming itself in the wax in the water bowl. The features were horrible, contorted in agony, twisted and deformed as if in excruciating pain. The hideous mouth and thin lips were moving slowly. There was no sound other than a brief 'plop', like a goldfish taking in air. The temperature inside the room had dropped despite the roaring flames. Lee could see the mist from his nervous panting circle and disappear in front of his face. They were all shivering.

Silently the bulbous lips of the monstrous wax face continued to move. As the mouth contorted, the mirror's surface began to fog outwards from the centre as if congealed in icy breath. The shroud on the misted glass began to dissolve, revealing a shimmering silhouette of Whitby Pavilion perched high on the West Cliff. It was as if they were gazing at it through thick smog. The image of the large red-brick façade was fading to show hundreds of black-clothed goth figures of all shapes and sizes streaming into the main auditorium. Then the smiling face of Katsumi appeared among the throng. She looked exactly the same as her student card, happy and relaxed. Quietly, a driving synthesiser rock beat began to filter into the room, enveloping the four watchers. Katsumi was dancing freely, her body moving rhythmically to the heavy beat. The band were obviously rocking the place, judging by the excitement on the faces of all those around her. The booming bass notes rattled the table, making the water bowl ripple and the wax face contort even more. Lyrics poured out smoothly from the smart singer on the stage, dressed in a stylish long black jacket and open cream shirt, and the crowd were on their feet. Then the music faded and the images in the mirror changed.

Katsumi was now on her own outside the building, clutching a small pink piece of paper in her hand and reading it over and over again. She smiled at the approaching figure. It was a man dressed in black and he embraced her passionately. They began to walk arm in arm on the cliff-top path above the beach. The man looked unsteady on his feet and was quite obviously very intoxicated. He seemed to be looking around, making sure they were on their own.

Once they'd walked out of sight of the main road, he grabbed her roughly and pulled her to him. Katsumi was trying to push him away but the more she struggled the tighter his grip seemed to be. Now she was on the ground, struggling underneath the man, kicking desperately, trying to escape. He put his hand over her mouth and ripped off her skirt, forcing his body between her legs. As her raped her, she was sobbing and writhing in agony, tears streaming down her face. The man tore off more of her clothing, the lacy fabric shredding under his strong grip. Katsumi's naked skin shone palely in the glow of the distant streetlights. Desperately she rolled and kicked, fighting against the bulk of the dark figure. With a last agonising effort, she finally pulled free.

Then she was running ... running blindly on into the night. The man was chasing hard just behind but she kept pounding forward, her hands reaching out frantically into the black darkness ahead. Then she was falling ... down ... down ... down ... onto the jagged rocks below. In her panic, she had run straight off the cliff top and fallen to the rocky beach below. The man stared down at her body. It looked like a broken rag doll, her skin cut from head to foot. He made an urgent call on his mobile phone and stood wringing his hands in worry until two other huge shadowy figures joined him carrying spades. Now they were digging, piling the sand in a growing mound to the side of the deep hole. They picked up her naked body between them and threw it carelessly in the hole, kicking sand from the mound over the corpse. For a brief second the headlights from a passing truck on the coast road silhouetted the three men. The horrified watchers in the room could clearly see their two visitors from earlier in the day, but the third man remained plunged in shadow.

The milky body in the grave was motionless, thick sticky blood oozing from the cuts caused by the sharp rocks. Then the disfigured girl's eyes sprung open. Her broken mouth contorted in agony. Sand was slipping into her throat choking her. She let out a piercing, haunting scream. Katsumi Kamo was being buried alive.

Then there was silence and the images were gone. Small cracks began to form in the Victorian mirror, spiralling outwards from the centre. With a huge crash it exploded into a thousand pieces, firing sharp shards of glass throughout the room. They were all screaming now. Flying fragments cut through their flesh and broke bloodily on the walls. The fire and candles guttered out, and they were plunged into utter darkness.

CHAPTER 16

THE MIDNIGHT FEAST

The rapid breathing of the four friends rasped through the bleak darkness. No one dared move – they were all listening intently, trying to figure out if they were alone or had been joined by some unearthly presence. Turner could feel the blood trickling down his face, and his forearms were wet with a combination of nervous sweat and more blood. He couldn't tell how badly he was injured nor see any of his companions.

As his eyes adjusted to the darkness, he slowly began to make out details of the scene swathed in the pale-blue moonlight from the window. The light was just enough for him to spot the matchbox under the table. Slowly and carefully he eased forward, opened the box and struck a match on the underside of the table.

The sudden bright flash blinded him for a second; then he raised the sizzling yellow flame up to eye level and looked around. Lee and Sandra were clinging to each other and shaking, eyes staring blankly forward. Jade appeared more relaxed but he knew on the inside she'd be just as frightened as everybody else. Her job had trained her to be calm during a crisis and take control of her emotions. She was following this advice to the letter right now, but her hands were still shaking. To his relief, he could spot no other presence in the room. All of them were bleeding from cuts across areas of bare flesh. Lee seemed to be the worst; there was a nasty gash diagonally across his forehead. The fading match began to burn his fingers, causing him to curse and drop it to the floor, so he lit another. Standing gingerly, he tiptoed his way to the light switch, trying his best to avoid the broken glass under his bare feet. He flicked the switch.

The room was a complete mess. Shattered pieces of the mirror were scattered everywhere, with the largest concentration spewed across the coffee table. Strangely, none had found their way into the water bowl. The white wax bobbing in the water was now a congealed muddle of white, with no trace of the disfigured face and its thin lips. Salt still neatly circled the ivory carving of the mask seller. It seemed exactly as it had been with the amber-coloured carving of Katsumi's distorted features at its feet.

'Look ... she's back.' Jade was pointing to the amber mask. 'I think her soul is trapped or bound by the netsuke somehow. When we summoned her spirit form, it couldn't cross the circle of salt. Goodness knows what would have happened if we hadn't had that for protection.' Her voice was remarkably matter of fact and Turner marvelled at her ability to keep a level head. Salt had been an anti-demonic talisman in many of the stories he'd read researching for his work. He vaguely remembered the superstition of wearing a bag of salt around the neck for protection by the accusers at the medieval witch trials. He'd always dismissed them as old wives' tales and pure fantasy. Now he'd seen its power to hold back spirits first-hand he finally understood. What else in his ancient textbooks was true? he worried to himself silently.

Sandra had started to clean up Lee's wounds using a first-aid kit from the bathroom. He looked comical wearing a huge dressing like a surgical bandana across his forehead. Methodically she wiped and dressed the worst cuts on the others and then turned her attention to the room. She popped into Lee's bedroom and came back wearing a thick pair of his black leather winter gloves and carrying the waste bin. Carefully she swept up handfuls of the shards of broken mirror and put them noisily in the bin. Lee was just looking at Turner, mouthing 'What the hell?' over and over, before signalling him to the landing for a private chat.

'Nathen, what the hell was that? C'mon, man, I've seen you do some scary crap but this is off the scale. What are you up to, man? There's got to be easier ways to get into Jade's pants. I mean c'mon.' The two friends stood alone outside the room where they couldn't be overheard.

'It's not me! I swear on my life, this is not me! Lee, this is bloody real and I'm as freaked as you,' he answered, holding Lee's gaze steadily.

'OK, if it's not you, swear on Kyle's life – then I know you're not lying. And show me your bloody hands, so I know you haven't got your fingers crossed when you say it!' Lee demanded, still not accepting what he said. Turner had played this childish game with Lee when they were school kids, saying his promises and word didn't count if he crossed his fingers when he said them.

'I swear to you on Kyle's life. I promise you on everything I hold dear that this is nothing to do with me,' he said holding out his open palms in front of him.

'Crap,' Lee muttered quietly and stared at the floor, lost in thought.

Turner could see through the crack in the door that Jade

was now holding the bin as Sandra carefully scoured the floor for glass fragments.

'I've got to ring Joe, I mean Detective Inspector Stewart.' Lee was making a move to grab his phone. 'He's never going to believe this one. If what we've seen in that bloody mirror is true, then there is a girl's body buried out somewhere under the cliffs near the pavilion.' Whitby Pavilion was built at the top of the West Cliff with superb views out to sea. During the summer season, it was a hive of activity with bands and family entertainment shows. The last thing Whitby Tourist Board needed right now, in the height of the season, was to find a disfigured corpse of a young girl buried beneath it.

Lee headed into his bedroom, closed the door and pulled out a plastic flower from a vase on his windowsill. He banged the hollow stem until a thin joint fell into his open palm. Sitting on the bed he pulled the cheap lighter from the bowl of peanuts on the side dresser before quickly lighting his spliff. He inhaled deeply, desperately trying to overcome the shock and fear he'd felt over the last hour. After another deep drag and more clouds of acrid smoke circling his head, Lee was fumbling with his smart phone screen and dialling a number.

Lee knew the police station on Spring Hill would be closed at this time of night so he rang the local police enquiry line and spoke to the duty sergeant. During his Hep Cats days having numbers for all the local out-of-hours police services had saved him from serious trouble more than once.

'Police,' said a flat emotionless voice at the end of the line.

'Is Detective Inspector Stewart on duty this evening?' asked Lee politely, a slight tremor in his voice.

'Who's calling, please?' The tone was flat and bored and

rapidly rustling through papers in the background.

'Lee, it's Lee Melone.' He always found it best to answer exactly what you were asked with the police – no more and no less.

'Oh, hey Lee. It's Tony Coppenger. How are things?' asked the now friendly and positively enthusiastic voice. Tony had been a big fan of the Hep Cats and tried to pull crowd control or public order duty for all of the gigs he could when they were touring. They'd struck up a friendship over the years and had many detailed discussions over things like Big Mama Thornton and Lonnie Johnson's blues styling – such is the way of blues aficionados the world over. After exchanging the usual polite catch-up greetings, Tony found that Stewart was covering nights again so should be on duty already. He patched him through.

'Hurricane, that really you? Past your bedtime, isn't it? What can I do for you at this godforsaken hour?' the surprised voice of Stewart said rapidly down the line. Lee knew Stewart couldn't have had much sleep. He'd already worked through the previous night and then covered the morning suicide at Oswin Hall.

Lee explained as best he could. He said he'd found out that there might have been a murder some time ago of a young Japanese lady, and her body was buried near Whitby Pavilion. He thought it had happened during one of the goth festivals but didn't know when. Thinking it best to leave out the bit about how he knew all this, he simply asked if Stewart could call around and talk to him and his housemates about it later. Together they could explain everything properly. To his relief Stewart listened and took him seriously enough to offer to call round after he'd made his next visit.

'I've got to cover a domestic down in Filey. Probably take me a couple of hours or so but I could get to you between midnight and one maybe – is that too late?' Lee wasn't expecting anyone in the house to get much sleep tonight so he gratefully accepted the offer.

By the time he was off the phone the lounge had been tidied and Turner was back inside sitting and talking with the girls. Lee joined them after dousing his room with strong air freshener and hiding the waste from the spent spliff. They'd all realised they were starving – they hadn't eaten properly all day. Nobody felt like cooking so they agreed to take a walk into the harbour and see if they could find a late-night takeaway. If they were being truthful, they also wanted to get away from the house for a while.

It was a beautiful night, the full moon painting the dark cobblestone alleyways in a shimmering pale light. The streets were very quiet, with only a few dog walkers around and locals heading home from the pub. Their mood lifted immediately and Jade was asking all about the harbour and the town, and the others were gladly explaining Whitby's wonderful history. Talking together about anything other than what had just happened seemed to be the perfect antidote to the fear they all felt. They were merrily engaged in colourful tales of eighteenth-century smugglers and their bawdy drinking and gambling habits when the unmistakable scent of fish frying hit them. It wrapped around them, engulfing them in a beautiful aroma of sweet crunchy batter and the sea. Kyle bounded ahead, following the scent to the distant sign that said simply 'Fish and Chips'. The black front of the takeaway was illuminated with a comforting blue light above a board covered in celebrity endorsements for the quality of the food inside. Next door the blackened face of the closed restaurant said 'Mandy's – best Fish and Chips in town', and meant it. Everybody in Whitby knew Mandy's on Church Street. Fresh fish were collected every morning from the best catches up and down the east coast and then covered in a secret beer-batter recipe before being fried in beef dripping. There was no low fat, health-conscious option here – this was old-school flavour at its very best. Mandy herself was serving at this late hour; she'd sent the rest of the staff home. As her flat was above the shop she often worked late then staggered up the stairs to bed, ready to do it all again the next day. Mandy Phillips had been a blonde bombshell in her day – big hair and big boobs bopping along to New Romantic music in the 1980s around every club she could find. She had slept her way round most of the DJs in the area before finally settling down with a chef from Doncaster who was working at one of the local restaurants. He'd eventually left her for a younger model and headed down south to seek his fortune, leaving Mandy with a load of debt and a broken heart. Firing all her energy into creating the fish and chip business had helped her cope with the loss. Ten years later, she had the best food in town and a healthy bank balance. Her own hunger wasn't as easy to satisfy. With no kids to hold her back she was still racing through scores of men, looking for Mr Right to make her toes curl. Lee and Turner knew this all too well as she'd tried to bed both of them for many years. Mandy was positively disappointed to see the two ladies follow the two eligible bachelors into the shop.

'Hey Lee, Nathen – what the hell happened to you lot?

Been in a fight?' she said, gazing at the four figures crisscrossed with a variety of sticking plasters, and Turner limping slightly from minor cuts on his feet. They shook their heads collectively, 'no,' so she went on, 'I'm almost ready to close up but I'm sure I could squeeze you boys in.' She pushed her boobs together when she said 'squeeze' and they all laughed at the flirtatious gesture.

'Fish and chips with scraps four times open, please, Mandy.' Jade looked at Lee as if he'd grown another head.

'What language is this you're speaking, Lee? Is this some secret English food code kept from foreigners?' Jade watched Mandy nonchalantly take the order and start to put it together. She was more of sushi-bar girl back home and kept her home-cooking to more traditional Japanese recipes. Lee explained the code.

'No,' Lee was laughing, 'with scraps means scraps of batter that fall off the fish and are collected – look.' And he pointed to a pile of crunchy batter piled high in the corner of the shiny steel warming cabinet. 'And open just means don't wrap them up – we'll eat them as we walk.'

'Oh, I see.' Jade was feeling a little embarrassed at her ignorance. When Lee smothered her steaming package of food in salt and vinegar she just accepted the ritual and enjoyed the rising aroma of the seasoned food. In high spirits, they headed into the street with Mandy calling 'anytime boys' after Lee and Turner and pushing her boobs together again in a lewd gesture.

They gobbled hungrily at the delicious food panting with their mouths open as the freshly fried chips proved hotter than expected. Biting through the crunchy batter exposed the soft white flesh of the fish that literally melted in their mouths, leaving a beautiful creamy flavour of the sea behind. The fear and craziness from the house seemed a lifetime ago, and they wandered happily along the East Pier, watching the waves froth and crash underneath them. Jade linked her arm with Turner's and gave him a little squeeze. He squeezed back and turned to see her beautiful face highlighted in the soft moonlight. Without thinking, he kissed her full on the lips, feeling the warmth of her body press against him. Or so he thought. It was actually the warmth of her fish supper that she'd swung between them in her surprise. The crushed meal caused more laughter, and she tossed it into a nearby bin before telling Turner she was now owed half of his remaining food. The pair of them walked on, arm in arm, sharing the paper-wrapped meal, laughing and giggling as they went.

Lee nudged Sandra to look at them. He had never seen Turner so happy with a woman. Now that he'd realised she wasn't actually crazy, he was warming to the partnership between them. They turned and headed back, Kyle greedily robbing scraps of food, his tail wagging madly. Mandy had closed up and the shop was completely dark on their return. The upstairs apartment light was on and there was a vision of two people embracing passionately silhouetted through the thin curtains. Lee nudged Turner to look, realising Mandy had got yet another guy snared in her flat.

Kyle bounded ahead down the now empty street, pepped up from his late snack. He turned the corner into the alleyway that led to the front door and waited expectantly on the doorstep. The others weren't far behind and Lee unlocked the heavy kitchen door and flicked on the light as Kyle pushed through ahead.

'PFFT!' came the sound of air rapidly escaping, and the dog fell to the floor motionless, a silver dart with red flocking sticking from its neck.

'Shut the door!' Roby commanded from the other side of the kitchen, quickly reloading the dart gun he'd shot the dog with. Pearson held the other gun over by the door and waved them rapidly inside.

Roby arced his dart gun across the four terrified friends. 'There's enough tranquilliser in these guns to stop an elephant. Do exactly what I ask or you'll be joining the dog.'

CHAPTER 17

HOUSE OF PAIN

Roby motioned the four upstairs. The lounge had been rearranged with the kitchen chairs now facing each other in a circle in the middle of the room. The coffee table and its contents had been pushed against the fireplace, and the settees and lounge chairs pushed flush against the opposite wall. This created a space all around the central chairs, front and back.

Roby motioned Turner to one of the chairs, training his weapon between the middle of the room and the group. Turner sat down heavily and Pearson roughly bound his wrists to each arm of the chair with silver gaffer tape. He repeated this for Lee and pulled his chair directly opposite the already bound figure. The two girls were ushered into the far corner of the room by the window. Pearson gave them a lewd smile and licked his lips as he taped both of their feet together at the ankles so one couldn't move without the other. Then he methodically taped their hands behind their backs and wedged them upright in the corner before forcing another piece of the sticky silver tape across their mouths.

'Now we're all comfortable, boys and girls, perhaps we can continue our little chat from this morning.' Roby was frighteningly calm and businesslike, putting his dart gun on the floor and sitting in one of the chairs between the two friends. Pearson stood blocking the door, his wide squat frame filling the opening.

143

'You have something of ours, and we want it back. We found this downstairs.' He waved the carved black wooden box slowly from side to side under Turner's nose. 'A very good pal of mine gave this little trinket box to a special lady friend. It has this secret compartment. Look …' He tilted the box upside down, showing that they had removed the hidden interior again after Jade had put it back. So the thugs knew its secret as well, Turner thought. 'Now, this lady friend used to keep things in here. Private things. Things no one else should see. But now they're gone, and we think you lovely people have stolen them. Now, that's not very nice, is it?' He glowered menacingly at the bound housemates. 'One of these things was a note, a simple note on a pink piece of paper. No use to anybody and very private between the pair of them. You wouldn't want to steal someone's personal correspondence, now would you?'

Turner was thinking furiously about the contents of the hidden compartment. He remembered the torn pink paper note with the badly drawn heart and kisses and the scribbled request for Katsumi Kamo to meet someone at the 'usual place'. Now finally, he thought he understood. The vision in the mirror must be of that tragic meeting and the note linked the man, this gorilla's so-called pal, to the crime. He'd seen the bullies in front of him clearly in the vision in the mirror – they'd helped the man bury the body. Somehow the note must incriminate them, and Turner realised despairingly that they were all in real danger.

Roby nodded at Pearson, who walked steadily from the doorway to stand directly behind Lee. 'Now, just so you know how important this is to us, we'll give you a little taster of what's to come if you don't help us.' Roby's eyes gleamed and he was positively excited. Pearson bent down and removed a short copper pipe from his boot and slipped it over the little finger on Lee's right hand. It looked to Turner like the piping plumbers use and he watched horrified as Pearson bent back slowly on the tube and Lee began to scream until there was a sickening crack. Lee passed out.

Turner played for time. In truth he had no idea where the note was now; they'd been focused on the little ivory netsuke and disregarded it. 'Look, we don't know anything. I don't even know who you are. It's not my box; it's from the hotel. How would I know it had a secret space? Leave Lee alone – if you want to hurt someone, use me,' he blurted out, sweat pouring down his face.

'OK, if that's what you want.' Roby stood up calmly and slowly, and then punched Turner hard in the face, breaking his nose. Blood streamed down from his damaged nostrils and splattered thickly onto his shirt. Turner was thankful that the bright red of his shirt was concealing how much blood he was losing as the girls were already beginning to freak out in the corner. He realised bizarrely that the cartoon cliché of seeing stars flashing in front of your eyes was true – there were hundreds of the little buggers swimming in front of him now.

'If you know nothing about it, how come the hidden compartment is empty? We know there was something in it – the box used to rattle. Now look.' As Roby shook it vigorously from side to side there was no sound from the carved box. 'Hear anything, psychic boy? You're a bloody liar!' This time, he slapped Turner hard across the left ear. 'Now, where's the note?'

Lee's little finger was already swollen and purple. 'We want our property back. I'm not a patient man, Mr Turner, so you have ten seconds before we break another finger. Ten ... nine ... eight ...'

Pearson deftly slipped the tube on Lee's third finger.

'... Two ... one ...' Then there was another huge crack and Lee was screaming again. Pearson was positively beaming and having the time of his life.

Turner was struggling to breathe through his shattered face and feeling powerless to help his friend. His heart pounded in his chest and the metallic taste of the blood in his mouth was making him feel sick. Jade was the only one who would know where the note was and there was no way he was going to allow her to be questioned. It surprised him how strongly he felt about protecting this beautiful green-eyed stranger.

'Look, I don't know where this note or whatever is – all I got was the box. How do you know it hadn't been removed before I got it?' Blood was now congealing in his throat, making him cough and pant for air.

For the first time, Roby paused. It was true; Juliet Armstrong or her late husband could have removed the note. But she'd not said anything when they'd tortured her. The husband was a gossip and would definitely have told somebody about the secret compartment if he'd discovered it. No, there must have been things still hidden inside the box because they'd found that stupid little ivory figure sitting on top of the table when they broke in. They'd forced the back door that opened onto the raised garden from the first-floor landing. The back of Turner's house was on the steep slope of the East Cliff so, as was normal with these Georgian stone houses, the paved garden area is accessed from the first floor, with the ground-floor kitchen effectively built underground into the rock below. It had been a simple job for the two men to jump over the garden wall to access the back of the building.

Roby stood and roughly grabbed the carved ivory figure from the salt circle on the table. 'If you don't know about the inside of the bloody box, then explain this to me, bright boy. This piece of tat used to be in there as well.' And with that he cuffed Turner across the other ear, the sound of the blow exploding in his head. The figure was inches from Turner's blood-soaked face, and he could see the contorted amber mask of Katsumi Kamo staring blankly and uncaringly at him from the base.

'It was just inside the box – sitting in the red lining,' he said, trying to think quickly.

'LIAR!' Roby blurted, punching Turner hard again in the face, fracturing his cheekbone this time. His face began to swell immediately, pushing up the flesh from under his left eye so that it was practically closed. Through his limited vision he could make out Pearson almost dancing with glee as he watched the savage beating. He was getting high on the violence.

Pearson chimed in from behind the mangled figure of Lee, 'There is no way that stupid little goth bitch would keep that in plain sight. It's some bloody family toy that is supposed to be important.'

'Keep your mouth shut. Our buddies here don't need to know anything about our lady friend, do they, you idiot!' Roby snarled at Pearson. He tossed the little figure carelessly back into the salt where it landed face up as if mocking Turner. 'So let's try again, shall we? Where is the note?'

His hand was around Turner's throat, choking him softly. Gradually the air was being cut from his body and he could sense the room spinning and fading in front of him. He felt this was the end and thought of Jade and what they would do to her, the horrible images flashing through his mind. Then he was back, the pressure had been released and he was desperately fighting for air. He could hear Lee shouting at him.

'Wake up! C'mon, wake up, man!' Lee was wrestling madly in his chair, rocking it unevenly back and forward. Pearson laughed hard and long when he lost his balance and fell, smashing onto his side, legs kicking aimlessly in the air. His hand was no longer recognisable as a hand; the two broken fingers were hugely swollen and purple, and pointing at wildly different angles.

But through the pain Lee was smiling. There'd been the sound of the kitchen door opening downstairs and the chime of a familiar voice shouting, 'Lee, Lee, you in here, Hurricane?'

CHAPTER 18

THE LONG ARM OF THE LAW

Detective Inspector Joe Stewart tiptoed carefully around the rigid figure of the dog in the kitchen, his ears straining for any sound from the house. He thought he could hear a very quiet whimpering and sobbing from above him, then a huge crash as if something heavy had fallen over. Edging his way slowly up the stairs a step at a time, he looked like a tweed-clad ninja in polished leather brogues.

All the lights in the house were on, which was a blessing, allowing him to pick out where he was walking, inch by slow inch. The only weapon he carried was an extendable black police baton, and he flicked it open expertly as he climbed. The door into the lounge on the first-floor landing was closed and there were large flakes of wood on the carpet at the end of the corridor. He eased his way silently forward and found that the back-garden door had been jimmied open with some force, causing an explosion of wood splinters to spread inside. The door had been crudely wedged closed again so that from the outside it looked perfectly normal.

He made his way back down the corridor and listened intently outside the lounge door. There was definitely somebody sobbing on the other side – it sounded like a woman, but it was somehow muffled. His ear touched the brown wood of the door, magnifying the noise, and he picked up a man moaning softly then gargling for air as if he was having difficulty breathing. Throwing caution to the wind he kicked the door open violently, shouting, 'Police, don't move,' and raising his baton high in the air.

What he saw in the room took his breath away. Straight in front of him, Turner was taped to a chair, his torso covered in thick congealed blood. The psychic's head lolled to one side, and he seemed barely conscious as he gasped for breath. Lee Melone was flat on the floor opposite him and one of his hands was a grotesque mess of purple flesh. Lee wasn't moving and from this distance Stewart couldn't tell if he was alive. In the far corner, two girls were taped together, their eyes wide with fear. Stewart recognised one as being the girl he'd seen with Lee that morning, but he had never seen the other one before. Both were sobbing, and their mascara had run, making their faces a bizarre clown's mask of smudged black lines and blusher. The wide tape across their mouths restricted their breathing, and the effort was obvious on their flushed faces. Two more chairs sat innocently in the middle of the room, and the nearest one had what looked like a black paintball air gun carelessly discarded underneath. No one else was visible in the room.

'Police, don't move,' he shouted into the room again from the doorway and got no response from the traumatised inmates. The girls' heads were nodding forward furiously towards the doorway and he called over, 'It's OK – we'll have you out of here in a jiffy.' Long experience had taught him not to rush into situations like this without thinking first, so he stayed put, re-evaluating the scene. Nothing changed. He felt safe enough to go and retrieve the air gun from under the chair. Quickly, he ran to the chair and grabbed it in his free hand. Up close he could see it was some type of dart gun with a silvery dart loaded in the barrel.

The door slammed shut behind him and Roby stood glaring next to Pearson, who had his dart gun aimed directly at the policeman's head. They'd been hiding behind the open door, out of sight from the corridor. Instinctively, Stewart spun around at the noise and pulled the trigger on the dart gun, hitting Pearson square in the chest with its silver dart. Clutching at his chest in surprise and clawing at his throat, he fell heavily to the floor. The strong tranquilliser was already shutting down his respiratory system, making him gag horribly. Roby knelt by his life-long friend and felt for a pulse.

'Bloody hell, I think you've killed him,' Roby exclaimed angrily at the policeman.

'He took me by surprise – shouldn't have been pointing a weapon at me, the nut job.' Stewart showed no remorse at all for his violent act.

Roby just shrugged and said, 'Sorry, boss. We got a bit carried away.'

'Where's the note? You've got it right? Please tell me you've got the sodding note!' he said, his temper rising as Roby was nodding an apologetic 'no' at him from across the room. Stewart moved close to the giant figure, glaring at him with fury in his eyes. Without warning he hit him hard across the face with the police baton and screamed at him, 'What do you mean, no? You've done all this for nothing?' Then he hit him again. The huge figure of Roby was cowering from this slightly built Scotsman brandishing a slim black baton and an empty dart gun in his hands. Stewart swapped his empty gun with Pearson's loaded one now lying discarded next to the prone figure.

'This is the second time you've messed it up. That scene at Oswin Hall was way too messy. Do you know how much squirming I had to do to convince the scene-of-crime boys it was a suicide? No, you don't, because you're a bloody idiot.' And he kicked him hard between the legs, his face red with fury. The vast frame of Roby dropped to his knees, shaking in pain, angry raised welts appearing across his cheek and forehead from the baton strikes. 'Does that hurt, big man?' As Roby nodded and grimaced 'yes,' Stewart shot him in the arm with the loaded dart gun. 'Good,' he said. Roby slumped heavily to the floor, the silver dart from Pearson's gun sticking out from the blue ink of his naval tattoo.

Turner was watching the horror of the beating with his one good eye. None of this made any sense. Stewart stood gazing down at the gigantic contorted frame of Roby, pushing him with his toe to check he wasn't moving. There was something about the policeman's standing profile that stirred his memory. Desperately he searched his thoughts, trying to identify the feeling that was gnawing at him. With a sudden dread he remembered the mirrored vision. The figure that met Katsumi Kamo outside the pavilion was not a huge man; it was a much smaller person ... it was Detective Inspector Joe Stewart.

He began to buck wildly in his chair, trying to rip free of the tape. Exhausted from the effort, he collapsed back, breathing noisily through his bloody and battered face. Then his world went black.

CHAPTER 19

GOTHS AND ROBBERS

The smell of death and human misery hung over the room. Stewart towered over the slumped figure of Turner.

'Wake up, Turner. We need to talk.' The voice broke through the black mists of his mind. Slowly, he lolled his head upright again, the waves of pain washing over him like jagged knives. Turner's face was almost unrecognisable. What used to be his nose was a flattened bloody mush and the swelling from his cheek had now closed his left eye completely. The blood frothed and foamed on his lips as his shallow breathing forced more of the congealed blood from his throat to the surface. 'Look, Turner, I've always had a soft spot for you. You know that, right?' A blink of acknowledgement was the best he could do. 'I just need a little help, that's all. I've lost something very important, and I need it back. It's a small pink piece of paper, this big.' And he mimed something around the size of a box of cigarettes with his hands.

'Why is it so ... special ...' Turner slurred through the aching torment of his shattered face.

Stewart pulled up a chair, put his weapons on the floor and carefully looked at the battered figure in front of him. The amount of blood he could see and the pallor of his skin suggested the psychic didn't have long to live. The detective had seen enough people close to death to know. Behind him, Lee looked to be unconscious or dead, and the two girls were too far away to hear anything he said. Stewart thought it might do him good to confess to a dying man after holding such a secret burning inside him for so long.

As a child he'd learnt to bottle things up. Life in the Highlands of Scotland had proved a tough existence for him back in the sixties. Elsewhere, free love and liberal views spread like a cancer across the Western world. Not so for him. His puritan father found such things an abomination and even talking about them would result in a severe beating at the end of his belt. In truth, most conversations with his son usually ended this way, using some ridiculous excuse or another to justify his sadism. His mother had been too terrified to stop the physical abuse, making it easier on herself by simply turning a blind eye. As an only child, there was no one to share the burden, so he'd turned to fantasy writing and movies to escape the prison of his childhood. His obsession with powerful figures and all-conquering monsters served to feed his father's rage even more. In his imagination Stewart thought that if he were like his monster heroes from the movies, then the blows would mean nothing to him. He often imagined himself as some devilish demigod who could do anything to anybody without consequences. And so were sown the early seeds of Joe Stewart, the psychopath. He leant close to Turner, the words flowing out like a cascading waterfall.

'I'm going to tell you something awful, Turner. But I need to explain. I'm not a bad man; I've just been unlucky. I never meant any harm on anybody.' Turner glimpsed over his shoulder at the two prone men and had some doubt believing that. 'When I first came down here thirty-two years ago in the early 1980s, there were loads of those frilly shirted New

Romantic types kicking about,' he began, 'and we were at war in the Falklands. Thatcher was in her element, trying to cripple the unions and the power of the working man. I was broke – a police constable's salary was certainly not enough to support my ambitions.'

'By chance I was assigned beat duty at the harbour. This was in the days when bobbies did walk the streets, not like now when they do it using cameras and sit behind a desk all day. That's how I met these two,' he said, gesturing in the direction of Roby and Pearson's prone figures.

'During a night patrol I happened to spot them doing something very suspicious on a fishing boat in the marina. They were emptying a lobster pot on the deck but the only thing that fell out was a plastic case covered in sand and seaweed. Now, I'm no nature lover, but even I know what a bloody lobster looks like and that wasn't it.' He grinned to himself, enjoying his tale.

'Turns out they were running a nice little smuggling operation between them. Well, this was too good a chance to miss. I offered them police protection for a cut and the odd case of whisky. It worked well for all of us and I kept enough evidence of their operation to lock them up for a long time if they ever crossed me. Plus they were handy with their fists and always willing to do the dirty work if I needed a bit of outside help on a case. Amazing how good violence is at getting confessions, eh?' He was looking at Turner for a response but nothing came except the rasping gasps of his laboured breathing.

'Anyway, time went on and I had settled into the community. After about ten years, I pretty much knew all the local villains and who held the power in the town. Then the goth festival came to town – it was fantastic for a guy like me and I made sure I pulled as many shifts as possible on the first one. After working all afternoon, I got changed and headed to Oswin Hall for a refreshing drink or three. That's when I saw a vision of such beauty, it made my head spin.' Stewart closed his eyes as if visualising the memory.

'She was simply stunning, sitting on her own in the bar, dressed in a black cotton and lace dress with a red high collar. Her oval brown eyes and soft skin stirred my lustful imagination. As a single guy I had nothing to lose so I tried my luck at talking to her. Turns out we were into the same movies so the conversation flowed easily. She told me her roommate was supposed to be with her but had got sick. Now on her own in a strange town, she was glad for some company. I think she was a history student or something at Leeds but I can't remember. She was worrying about some little ivory figure she'd brought with her being stolen, as there was no secure place to keep valuables in the hotel in those days. It was supposed to be pretty precious to her but just looked like a little hunchback carrying a load of masks to me. Women, eh?' He looked over at Jade and Sandra writhing in the corner. He hadn't noticed the ivory carving discarded amidst the salt on the coffee table.

'Turns out I had just the thing – a carved puzzle box with a secret compartment, great for hiding things. This one here,' he said, picking up the black box from the floor where Roby had left it. 'I told her she could keep hold of it until she left, and showed her how to open it. I've had it since I was a kid – used it to store things I didn't want my parents to see.

Carpenter friend of my mother's put it together. It's a really clever design. Proved pretty useful for me, and the boys too,' he continued, pointing at the two thugs on the floor. 'Great way for us to pass private messages about our little smuggling sideline. Anyway, that's another story.' He leaned back and lit a cigarette, blowing the thick smoke calmly up towards the ceiling.

'We took a walk up to the pavilion in the moonlight. It was wonderful, felt like I'd known her for years. I desperately wanted to see her again so we agreed to meet the next day at the same place up on the cliff top. Trouble was, I'd forgotten what shift I was on so agreed to leave her a note at reception in the hotel confirming everything. Most of the morning I was with nutjob over there,' he continued, pointing over at Roby with his foot, 'at his harbour master's office. I used one of his pink council receipt sheets to write a note to my new friend – Katsumi Kamo was her name but I called her Kat. Just seemed to fit somehow. I said I'd meet her at our usual spot – which was a bit presumptuous as we'd only been that one time. My little joke I guess, hoping this would become a regular thing. In case she'd forgotten, I drew a little map at the bottom of the paper showing the place and left it at the hotel while I was on my rounds.' He was inhaling deeply on his cigarette, letting the smoke billow out of his nose in a steady stream. His gaze seemed distant as if he was lost in another time and place.

'Anyway, I'd gone to the bar again after work and got chatting with a few locals and lost track of time. I'd also lost track of how much I'd drunk. By the time I met Kat, she was anxious and thought I wasn't coming. I found her at the top of the cliff, reading over and over the map on the slip of paper to see if she'd got the place wrong. The paper was torn so I asked her what had happened. She told me she wanted to keep the part of the note with my message on as a keepsake of our friendship, hiding it in the box for safekeeping while she was here. I was delighted that she was so into me already.' He blew smoke hard into Turner's face to see if he was still conscious. He coughed blood in response so Stewart continued his story.

'I wanted to relive the closeness we'd felt the night before but in my drunken state I scared her as I tried to pull her close. She pushed me back and I lost my temper and pushed her to the ground. I'm not proud of what happened next … but I was drunk, you see … very drunk.' His eyes pleaded with Turner, who was just dazedly staring back at him with his one good eye.

'My lust took over, and she ended up running naked into the night with me chasing after her. Then she just disappeared. Literally gone, just like that. I searched in the dark before I figured out what happened. She'd fallen off the cliff and I could see the reflection of her pale broken body in the moonlight.' He began to cry. Softly at first then sobbing sadly. 'It was an accident. You understand that, right? She just ran …' He lit another cigarette and sat silently smoking, lost in his thoughts before a rattling cough from Turner jerked him back to his story.

'I panicked. So I rang the only two people I knew who would help me. They had as much to lose as me if they ratted me out – I'd make sure of that.' He gestured with his foot towards Roby on the floor. 'The big one's wife was sick, and he desperately needed the money he was making from the smuggling to pay for her care.' Stewart was taking great care not to mention Roby and Pearson by name in front of his psychic confessor. The less he knew about their identities the better. He didn't expect the psychic to live but years as a policeman had taught him to be cautious. Once Stewart had got the note back, anything he'd told Turner would be classed as hearsay, with nothing to back it up and link him to Katsumi Kamo's body if it was ever found. He knew any forensic traces would be long destroyed with the passing of the years. 'We found a remote spot under the cliff away from the tidal flow and buried her ...'

Stewart stopped talking and looked down at the floor as if ashamed. Slowly, he pulled himself upright and continued. 'You understand, don't you? It was an accident – what was I supposed to do? After a few weeks she came through on the police network as a missing person but back then the technology and co-operation between forces were rubbish, so they never traced her to Whitby. As far as everyone was concerned, she'd left the town and gone missing on her way back home. We'd already cleared all traces from her room, anyway.' The detective now seemed impressed with himself and his ability to cover up his horrific crime.

'It's been twenty years and not a day has gone by that I don't think of her. Always waiting for the body to be discovered; waiting for it to destroy my life. I've got a family now. What do you think this would do to my wife? The only thing left that ties me to her is that note. We never did find the bloody thing. It's got my handwriting on, don't you see? I've never even admitted to knowing her. Last thing I need now is a load of awkward questions and then some bright spark figuring out she never left Whitby. When I was told my carved puzzle box had turned up, I just wanted to hide away and die. Can't you understand what it's doing to me? I need that note; I must have that note or my life is over.' He was pleading now, viewing himself as an innocent victim of circumstances.

Turner inhaled as deeply as he could, trying to speak, pain enveloping him, blood oozing from his mouth in thick drops. Stewart leant forward to listen as his voice came out in a thin whisper.

'She ... was ... still ... alive ...'

'What? What did you say?' He shook Turner, jolting him upright.

'Katsumi ... Kamo ... was ... still ... alive ... when ... you ... buried ... her,' he repeated slowly, each word a major effort for his aching body. It was too much for Turner, and he drifted into unconsciousness.

Stewart was sobbing again now but much louder than before, his whole body rocking back and forward, wringing his hands in dismay.

CHAPTER 20

CLINGING TO LIFE

Jade and Sandra had watched on as Stewart held his one-way conversation with Turner. They couldn't hear what was being said but it looked like Turner had muttered something that caused Stewart to break down and weep. It seemed a truly extraordinary scene that a broken and bloody man on the edge of death had caused his torturer to sob with a few mumbled words.

Now Stewart seemed to be regaining his composure, his tears replaced with anger. He shook Turner's shoulders furiously, trying to wake him up, screaming at him, 'You're a liar. How could you know? You're a bloody liar.' The same phrases over and over again. There was no response from the slumped figure. In fact, it looked like he was already dead before the policeman tried to revive him. Turner was deathly pale and covered in his own blood, his nose and face a bulbous mess of pulped flesh.

Stewart glared around the room. Lee was on his side, motionless, and the only signs of life were the two girls propped whimpering in the corner. His mind reeled with what he had done in his fit of rage. He must think – somehow he needed to cover his tracks. The broken door on the landing would easily cover a story about a forced break-in. The plan with Roby and Pearson had been that he'd show up as the conquering hero and arrest them before letting them go sometime later, on a technicality he would have manufactured. That was before the stupid buggers had given in to their craving for violence. All he wanted was a box containing a simple piece of paper, and it had caused all this.

He picked up the carved box carelessly discarded on the floor and walked under the light to examine it. The secret compartment had already been removed and there was no sign of any slip of paper. Perhaps he was wrong. Katsumi Kamo may have lied and not kept the note. Or maybe it had been destroyed; it certainly wasn't here. Looking out the window, he could see that the streets were quiet and no one had overhead the screaming and shouting. So far, he was in the clear.

Stewart reached into his pocket and pulled out another cigarette before sitting down again in the middle of the room. The girls were wriggling and pulling furiously at their bonds, trying desperately to free themselves. It was impossible for them to stand with their legs bound together, and with their hands behind their backs there was no way of levering themselves upward anyway. Stewart watched them struggle, safe in the knowledge they couldn't escape. He puffed smoke into the room, his mind racing, chin on his hands and his eyes fixed on the girls. The Asian girl reminded him of Katsumi in some ways but this one was older and more lithe and strong. The green flowered shirt she was wearing exposed a tempting glimpse of bare thigh as she wriggled uncomfortably from side to side. Smooth muscles in her legs rippled as she wrestled on the floor and lustful thoughts started filling his head. But he knew he couldn't touch either of them. Leaving traces of his sexual activity at a crime scene with a couple of strangers just wasn't tenable. The problem was, they'd witnessed the whole thing and no doubt would give damning accounts of his part in the evening. As he inhaled smoke deep into his lungs he knew the only way out was to kill them all. Then a cover story of how he'd discovered the violent break-in and was forced to kill Roby and Pearson in self-defence should work perfectly. With them all dead and no one to contradict him, he was confident he could make his imaginary tale stick with his superiors.

The only problem was how to kill them – he needed to find refills for the guns. He tossed away the spent cigarette and moved to Roby's prone body. After a few moments frisking his pockets, he found what he was looking for – a handful of steel cylinders that simply said 'WARNING – M99. Licensed veterinary use only' next to a small skull and crossbones, outlined in black. Quickly, he removed two of the silver darts and then began to load them into the empty tranquilliser guns on the floor.

Jade could sense what was coming from the violent psychopath and fiercely renewed her battle with the tape. Her hands were bleeding and she tried to show no emotion as a sharp shard of mirror glass sliced through the tip of her probing finger. When the thugs had moved the settees to the wall they'd uncovered areas of the floor the girls hadn't cleaned. Jade's violent wriggling had unwittingly moved the pair of them across the room just far enough to reach the virgin floor space and the jagged piece of glass. The wet blood trickled through her fingers, as she blindly sawed at the silver tape that bound her wrists. Her eyes were locked on the figure of the policeman still trying to figure out how to reload the guns and so far failing badly. She covered the noise of her slashing cuts by continuing to writhe side to side, rubbing her and Sandra's bound heels against the carpet. Sandra sensed Jade was up to something and turned to look at her with eyes pleading.

Stewart was getting increasingly frustrated with the guns. Before he could load the darts there was some sort of slide lock above the barrel that he just couldn't figure out. He'd been firearm trained but these airguns were totally different. It was an easy job to pull the trigger of a loaded gun but getting the dart in the right place was proving an impossible task. Sitting down again, he examined them more carefully. Each dart was a long silver cylinder the size of a large pen with a tailpiece of a red fibrous material. At the opposite end to the red flight, a thin needle, just like the tip of a hypodermic syringe, hid inside the steel cylinder. He figured the force of the impact must inject the drug somehow. So, he thought, if he could manually slam the dart hard enough into the women's skin it would have the same effect as firing the dart. Satisfied, he picked up two darts and walked over to them with death in his eyes.

Stewart had been sitting with his back to Jade, so she couldn't see what he'd done or picked up. As he turned she noticed the two darts in his hand and hastened her frantic efforts, cutting deeper into her skin in the process. The blood was making her grip slippery and she dropped the shard and couldn't find it again.

Stewart leaned over the two of them, the foul smell of stale cigarette smoke clinging to his tweed suit. He was calm. Worryingly calm. 'Nothing personal, ladies,' he said in a matter-of-fact way, raising his right arm high in the air. With a slam he brought the dart down hard onto Sandra's exposed shoulder. She tried to scream but the tape over her mouth stopped the sound, her neck muscles bulging with the effort. He studied her carefully, but she remained awake and terrified. 'Shit,' he said simply, and did it again. This time there was an audible crack as the force of the blow broke her left collarbone, causing her to lean awkwardly on that side. Still no effect – the toxic cocktail remained firmly in its metal shell. The darts were triggered only from a high-velocity impact, and his flailing attempt simply wasn't strong enough. 'Shit,' he said again and walked back to the centre of the room to re-think his approach. Puffing on yet another cigarette, he carefully went back over the guns. With a little cry of glee, he re-examined the loading catch and finally figured out how the missile was locked in place. With a huge sigh of relief that caused more clouds of stinking smoke to pour from his mouth, he loaded both guns.

Jade knew she was dead. As soon as he'd found the extra darts she knew it. Adrenalin coursed through her veins, blotting out the pain in her hands, as she pulled with all her strength to lengthen the tear she'd made in the tape. With a final loud rip her hands were free. She wrenched the strip of tape clumsily off her mouth.

'*Katsumi Kamo watashi wa watashi ni anata o yobidasu,*' Jade screamed, using the words from the mirror ritual to summon the spirit of Katsumi Kamo.

Stewart spun toward the sound of the tearing tape and shouted Japanese, recoiling in shock at Jade's bloody hands and mouth. The blood from her fingers had spread all over her cheeks as she'd fumbled to release the strip of tape on her face. She looked like someone had slashed her face repeatedly.

From the centre of the room the policeman was reliving the horrible vision of Katsumi Kamo's broken body on the rocks. Shuddering as the grisly memories clouded his brain, he shouted, 'Shut the hell up. Just shut the hell up, won't you? I'm going to make this as quick as possible. It's not my fault, you know. I didn't want this.' His gaze fixed on Jade as he desperately tried to erase the visions flooding his mind.

'*Katsumi Kamo watashi wa watashi ni anata o yobidasu,*' Jade screamed again as loud as she could.

A smell of rotting flesh filled the room, causing Stewart to wrinkle his nose in surprise. Behind him on the coffee table, a light mist was rising from the figure of the mask seller. Up and up it rose, cascading backwards off the ceiling and down again to the little ivory carving. The temperature in the room was dropping rapidly, and he began to shiver violently, the guns shaking in his hands. The small amber mask at the foot of the carving was dissolving into the mist, turning it blood red. Swirling and turning, twisting into grotesque patterns as it went, a thin pair of pale legs took shape in the crimson vapour. Now a torso, then the naked breasts of a teenage girl, then thin spidery arms. Higher and higher the smog wrapped the emerging spectral body. Slowly a face was taking shape. A horrid semblance of a face, contorted and bloody with hollow black eyes. There stood the pale weak frame of the spirit of Katsumi Kamo. Without warning, huge cuts opened all over the frail figure and spurted thick blood onto the table. The tortured face screamed; a piercing, shattering wail of a noise that dropped Stewart to his knees in fright.

'I ... see ... you ... Stewart ... I ... see ... you.' The spectre's bloody hands pointed straight at him, desperately trying to reach out and grab hold of his arm. The ashen and bloody frame tried relentlessly to move forward but couldn't leave the table. With arms scrabbling in front, and mouth formed into a grotesque snarl, the hollow black gaze never left the policeman.

Stewart turned to face the horrific vision and automatically fired both dart guns. The two silver streaks travelled straight through the frightening ethereal frame, now dripping in blood, and landed noisily into the wall behind. He knelt, unable to take his gaze from the sickening shape. Then he recognised the features of the towering spirit. 'Kat, is that you? Kat, I'm so sorry ...'

Jade watched the scene intently next to a whimpering Sandra. She couldn't understand why the ghostly figure she'd summoned with her words seemed fixed to the spot. And then she saw it – the salt ring was holding it in place. The very ring they'd used for their protection now spelt their doom. The table was too far away for her to get to and, besides, Stewart was in the way. Jade dropped her head in defeat, finally accepting her fate from the corrupt cop. Not even the spirits could help her.

The horrible disfigured body that used to be the beautiful Katsumi Kamo was scrabbling in confusion like a cat on a leash trying desperately to get to a mouse. The bloody bony fingers scratched and scraped vainly at the frigid air, trying hopelessly to leave the surrounds of the table. Angry wailing filled the room, brimming with hatred and pure rage, twisting around, frantically searching for a way to get to Stewart. Then the searching hollow gaze noticed the salt ring and hissed. An ominous, furious hiss that sent shivers down Jade's spine. With its thin mouth curled in a snarl, the ghoul turned to face the large water bowl outside the salt. The hissing was louder now and mixed with a vehement guttural roar. Bubbles began to form around the solidified wax in the bowl and the surface began to boil and fizz. The mess of white wax was melting and re-forming rapidly into a rising column that was struggling to break free of the water's surface. Slowly, it wriggled upwards like an anaemic greasy worm and then spread to form the shape of Katsumi's twisted face and thin lips. The monstrous shiny white mask was staring at the detective and floating across the room to where he knelt, shaking in terror.

Instinctively, Stewart's arms reached up to cover his face and push away the hideous apparition. He began screaming uncontrollably, his entire body wracked with fear. Then the wax face pushed through his clawing fingers, re-forming as it went and sliding its molten features into his screaming mouth and down his throat. The noise stopped abruptly as Stewart clutched at his neck, his eyes bulging as he struggled for breath. The stench of burning flesh in the room was nauseating.

Stewart wriggled wildly on the floor, convulsing in agony, sweat pouring from every pore. Katsumi's spirit in the salt circle was smiling with a drooling black mouth, watching the writhing body convulse in pain. Stewart began to burn. Slowly at first then spreading outwards from his torso. With flickering sheets of red flame around him, he began to stumble blindly around the room towards the table. His clothes melted into his skin, and a sickening smell of overdone meat wafted towards Jade. Now Stewart was a raging inferno, his skin already blackening and crisping. His corpse fell forward and knocked over the table, toppling the little netsuke figure onto the floor and out of the salt ring. Now free to move, the pale wraith-like body stood directly over Stewart and grinned horribly. Slowly and methodically, it began to beat the blackened carcass, first the head, then the body. Blow after merciless blow hammered into the ashen relic that used to be the policeman. The sooty corpse cracked and disintegrated into a messy pile of dark-grey ash.

At last satisfied, Katsumi's spirit rose, then seemed to take a deep cleansing breath as though renewed now that its revenge was complete. As the pale spectral frame got to its feet, Jade could see the wounds on the face and skin beginning to close and heal. The black hollows on the face were no more and all traces of the dripping blood simply disappeared. Elegant amber eyes gazed at Jade and the mouth morphed into a beautiful smile. The elegant naked figure of Katsumi Kamo was floating above the floor, drifting around the room, taking everything in. Tilting its head at Turner's immobile body, it stopped as if studying him for a while. Slowly, the pale figure leant forward, placing a thin hand gently on his chest, cold eyes staring into his crumpled and bloody face. Jade feared the worst and expected him to disintegrate in a ball of flame.

'No, don't do it. He was trying to help,' she pleaded. The spirit turned and slowly stared towards the sound of the noise as if recognising Jade's presence for the first time.

'I ... know ... little ... one. Watch ...' The voice seemed to be coming from inside Jade's head. Sweet like trickling water, all sign of anger and malice long gone. Katsumi's ghostly figure seemed to be concentrating, all its attention focused on the broken psychic. Turner's chest began to rise and fall under the pale hand, slowly at first but there was definitely movement.

'He … will … live … but … he … can … never … be … the … same …' the voice inside Jade's head was saying. Breath was rasping painfully and slowly from Turner's mouth, then forming small freezing clouds of vapour around his head. 'Part … of … him … will … always … walk … with … the … spirits … now …'

Katsumi's spectral body, now healed and whole again, left Turner and glided gracefully into the centre of the room, smiling softly at Jade. Directly above, a bright white light formed, beaming its brilliant rays into every corner of the room. The revived spirit opened its arms gratefully and looked up happily into the vivid glare. Gradually, the thin frame began to dissolve into the light, the face now a picture of peace and tranquillity.

And then it was gone.

CHAPTER 21

DREAMS AND HEALING

Turner was dreaming. He was naked, sitting on a small stool next to a carved wooden washbowl. Steaming heat from a softly bubbling pool in front of him engulfed his nude body in a warm comforting glow. The large open pool was surrounded by the most beautiful view he had ever seen. He was on top of a mountain, looking down into a verdant valley with a rippling stream at its foot. The colours of nature were exploding everywhere, with deep greens joining delicate ochre browns amongst the thick forest that covered the hillside. A polished stone path marked the entrance to the pool topped by sprigs of tall rushes and a variety of red and yellow flowers. Jade was next to him, wiping his bare limbs with a small white linen cloth, slowly, inch by sensual inch. She was smiling, her rich black hair tied back tightly behind her. After each sweep across his skin she was rinsing the cloth in the washbowl before wringing it out and starting again. As he watched the gentle ritual he noticed that Jade was also completely naked. He began to blush as she caught him staring in admiration at her beautiful body.

'In Japan we are not ashamed of our bodies,' she reassured him, and added cheekily, 'and from what I've seen, you certainly shouldn't be ashamed of yours.' He automatically looked down between his legs and laughed – she had a wonderful way of making him feel at ease, and he relaxed as she continued wiping his skin gently with the cloth. He noticed a lot of pale white scars on her hands as she reached down to pull him from the stool and lead him to the water. Slowly, he stepped into the scalding water of the hot spring and allowed his aching muscles to unwind as he sunk lower into its vaporous depths. The strange blend of natural minerals dissolved in the water made it seem more like entering a hot soup rather than a hot bath. He could taste the saltiness on his lips, and it felt wonderful.

Jade moved opposite him and they both sat down on a natural rock shelf under the water, facing each other. She stretched out her athletic legs and began to slowly rub the soft sole of her foot against his thigh ...

The pain in his face jerked him upright shattering the beautiful erotic vision. He was in a small hospital room, propped upright in bed. Looking around, he could see a cannula taped onto his arm, feeding drugs into his body from a thin plastic tube connected to a transparent drip bag on a steel stand above him. The bag was empty. White dressings were taped to the centre of his face, making a triangular tent over the area around his nose, and two thin tubes passed through the bottom of the dressing, feeding oxygen from the copper pipes behind the bed. Turner felt like he'd been kicked in the face by a horse – a horse that was in a particularly foul mood. A thin blue and white hospital gown was tied neatly around him, spattered with blood here and there. Jade was asleep in a high-backed chair next to the bed, a paperback book spread open and face down on her lap. Both her hands were wrapped in white gauze bandages.

He was glad to be alive. The last thing he remembered was the snarling face of Detective Inspector Joe Stewart whispering his sordid confession into his battered face. Then he remembered about Lee, Sandra and Kyle. 'Jade, Jade, wake up,' he said, his voice strained, feeling the stitches under the bandages stretch painfully as he moved his mouth. Luckily, she was dozing lightly and responded to his voice immediately.

'You're awake!' she cried with glee. 'I thought we'd lost you.' Turner had been in a coma for four days before the medical team had agreed to operate on his nose. They saw no point doing a nose job on a dead man, so had waited until they thought he had a good chance of pulling through. The damage was so extensive that he had been transferred to a specialist plastic surgeon at Leeds Shire Hospital. The surgery took eight gruelling hours during which he'd clinically died twice on the operating table. Somehow his body had kicked back in, fighting for life as if he had an angel on his side helping him. That was three days ago, and he'd been unconscious since then, sedated heavily by morphine.

Turner's mouth was dry so Jade poured him a glass of water from the side table and let him take sips through a straw. He gagged when the cold liquid hit his throat, and she bent him forward tenderly until it had passed. The brief effort had exhausted him and waves of pain crashed over his battered body. Jade brushed back his hair. 'We'll talk later. You must rest now.' With that, he slumped back onto the pillows, panting and moaning softly. Jade pressed the buzzer for the nurse and watched as they expertly renewed his drip and calmed him until he drifted to sleep again.

… He was back at the hot spring, staring into Jade's beautiful green eyes and smiling face. She was completely oblivious to their nakedness and chatted gaily, the steaming water reddening her skin and flushing her complexion. A bird chattered loudly up in an overhanging tree, and Turner scanned the foliage to see a beautiful white and red plumed body and long feathered neck poking through the branches. His eyes continued scanning around the area until his gaze rested on the figure of a young woman. She was standing alone, higher on the hillside, dressed in a white kimono tied tightly at the waist with a red silken sash. Her face was happy and relaxed, and she looked down lovingly at the two naked bathers. He recognised her immediately as Katsumi Kamo …

Turner jolted awake again, sweating. The sight of Katsumi had returned the horror of his torture back to him, and he couldn't get back to sleep. It was dark outside and there was no sign of Jade. The nurses had left the night light on above the bed, so they could see him clearly from the open doorway rather than come in and disturb his slumber. Someone, probably Jade, he thought, had left a pile of the *Whitby Gazette*, the town's local newspaper, on the side table. He could see that some stories in the 'Breaking News' column had been circled in red pen, and assumed he was meant to read them. Intrigued, he slid them over onto the bed under the pale illumination and started reading:

Whitby Gazette, Tuesday Evening Edition
Breaking News – Guitarist Injured in Brutal Robbery

Local guitarist Lee 'Hurricane' Melone was found severely injured at his home in Prospect Place amidst what appears to be an attempted robbery gone wrong. A police spokesperson has confirmed that officers responding to a 999 call found seven people, including Lee Melone, in the property in the early hours of Tuesday morning. Three are believed dead, another critically injured and Lee and two others, thought to be women, are suffering from shock and minor injuries. Full details of the incident and identities of the other casualties have been withheld at this time, pending a detailed investigation.

The news that Lee was alive and the girls only had minor injuries filled his heart. He had feared the worst when he saw the bandages on Jade's hands. There was no mention of his dog, Kyle, which surprised him. Reviewing the date on the paper, he saw it was a week ago and panicked slightly. He had no memory whatsoever of anything from that time to now. Realising he'd completely lost a week of his life, he picked up the next paper anxiously, desperate for information:

Whitby Gazette, Wednesday
Breaking News – Local Psychic Fighting for Life

Nathen Turner, local personality and popular psychic medium, is fighting for his life at Scarborough Hospital today. His friend and roommate Lee Melone has confirmed that Mr Turner has extensive facial injuries and is not expected to last through the night.

175

Police have stated that he was found at the Prospect
Place murder scene yesterday but how and why he
was injured remains unclear.

So it had moved from a robbery gone wrong to a murder
scene in a day. The lack of detail was frustrating him and his
head was pounding. Still no mention of Kyle. The view he had
seen out of his hospital room window earlier didn't look like
Scarborough, so where was he now? Next to the short text
there was a small smiling photo of him and he recognised it
as one of his publicity headshots. He grabbed the next
newspaper, desperately searching for answers:

Whitby Gazette, Friday
Breaking News – Gruesome Body Recovered at
Whitby Pavilion

The mutilated body of a young girl has been found
buried on the beach above the high tide line
underneath Whitby Pavilion. This follows information
provided by local guitarist Lee 'Hurricane' Melone to
police on Wednesday as part of the ongoing Prospect
Place enquiry. The body is thought to be of an Asian
lady but her identity is not known at this time. Further
information is expected to be forthcoming next week
after forensic examination has taken place over the
weekend. Local psychic Nathen Turner, found critically
injured at the scene, has been transferred to Leeds
Shire Hospital for specialist surgery.

They'd found Katsumi Kamo! He didn't know it but under the bandages he was smiling at the news. Somewhere down deep inside he felt strange. All his life had been built on the belief that psychic phenomena were really a tissue of lies and deception. He'd made a good living from exploiting gullible people keen to believe in the improbable. What he'd seen in the last few days was certainly real enough, and he felt different somehow. Like his ordinary self wasn't listening or paying attention to his old beliefs; it was an eerie sensation and he wanted it to stop. Pushing away the bizarre emotions racing through his mind, he grabbed the last newspaper from the pile. This time the story was front-page news:

Whitby Gazette, Monday
Dead Detective Linked with Pavilion Body

Police have confirmed this morning that Detective Inspector Joe Stewart, found dead at Prospect Place last Tuesday morning, is linked with the suspicious death of the Asian girl discovered last Friday near Whitby Pavilion. Evidence has come forward from an unknown source that Stewart was with the girl on the night she died and investigations are ongoing to determine how she met her tragic end ...

Then the piece went on to give a brief biography of Stewart and the little that was known of the corpse. There were images of Stewart, Whitby Pavilion and the front of Turner's terraced house at Prospect Place. Turner guessed his housemates had found a way of giving the pink note to the police investigation team without revealing their supernatural helper. The simple task of reading had exhausted him, so he slumped back and gave in to his growing fatigue.

… He was dreaming again. Katsumi Kamo was smiling at him, her almond skin and ruby-red lips framed by long loose locks of black hair falling over her shoulders. It looked like she was dressed for bed in a short white kimono emblazoned with cherry blossom and open-toed sandals on her bare feet. They were in a small room with paper-and-wood-framed walls. She motioned him forward across the straw mats covering the floor to the corner of the room. Picking up a plain wooden crib, she lifted it so he could look inside. Cascades of white silk poured from the interior, revealing something lying in the bottom. It was small, light brown and slowly moving and stretching. It was a tiny baby, fast asleep in the nest of the soft material. Katsumi handed it to him with a slight bow …

'Wake up, you're bleeding again.' A concerned Jade was standing over him, dabbing tissues on his cheeks. As he dreamt, he'd rolled over on his side and opened the stitching around his nose. An hour later, he was re-sown, re-bandaged and re-medicated. It was the best he'd felt so far, the heavy drug cocktail numbing the raging pain in his face.

'I've been dreaming of Katsumi Kamo.' Jade was squeezing his hand through her bandages as he spoke. 'She keeps coming to me. But she's happy, healthy, smiling. I can't get her out of my mind.'

'You never will …'

'What do you mean? How could you know that?' He

forced himself upright against the pillows, leaning forward, trying to understand what Jade was saying.

'You died, Nathen. In that room. You died. She saved you.' Jade's eyes were soft and gentle, her bandaged hands reminding him of the reality of their ordeal.

'Don't be ridiculous. I'm alive, aren't I? In a hospital? They saved me, not some crazy evil spirit from god knows where.' Up to now he'd never accepted such things even existed outside of fiction or his bizarre book collection. Now, facing the reality that he was wrong, he felt frustrated and confused and it was coming out of him as anger.

'She's not evil – what happened to her was evil. Her spirit couldn't rest while her murderer roamed free. Now I know she's at peace; I saw her change in front of me. It was incredible … but …'

'But what? Don't tell me she's still out there and coming for me!' The anger was replaced with fear.

Jade laughed a little, which did nothing to calm Turner's shredded emotions. She could see the irritation building up inside him. 'Calm down and listen to me. Look at your chest – there, near the heart …'

Reluctantly he did as he was told and lifted the thin cotton hospital gown up over his body. Around his left nipple was a series of five wavy white lines marked out in thin scar tissue. They were difficult to see in the dim room so Jade pulled the overhead angle-light down so he could get a closer look. The scars appeared more like the outline of a white birthmark, and the skin inside the contours was slighter paler than the rest of his chest.

'There, see?' She splayed her hand over the marks. 'It's the outline of her handprint. She touched your chest and ... well ... erm ... you started breathing again.'

Realising for the first time that he wasn't wearing underwear, he rapidly pulled the gown back down. The embarrassed gesture caused them both to giggle a little, lightening the mood.

'I saw it all. Please believe me – she saved you, but ...'

'Another but! What now?'

'She said you'd never be the same. That you'd always have a part of you living in the spirit world. At least I think that's what she meant.'

'What the hell does that mean?' Turner was calmer this time but still finding it difficult to accept what he was being told.

'I don't know. I just know what she said to me before she disappeared. She was happy and healed. I don't think we'll ever see her again now that her soul is at peace.' There was no laughter now; Jade was deadly serious. She looked hurt by the way he was speaking to her. Realising how ungrateful he must appear after all he'd put her through, he felt ashamed. Needing time to think and take it all in, he rapidly changed the subject. 'What news on Kyle? There is no mention of him in the newspapers.'

'He was rushed straight to the emergency vets so was long gone before the newspapers got there. Luckily the dart had caught him in the soft scruff of his neck and not fully injected the dose. The vet gave him some antidote thing – here, I wrote it down.' She reached for a slip of paper in her jeans. 'M5050, or diprenorphine it was called - to reverse the effects. It still took him three days to wake up and he's not quite himself yet.

Lee's looking after him. Look, you need to rest. I'm not supposed to get you excited.'

Her very presence excited him but she was right; he could feel the heaviness in his body. Nodding meekly at her, he allowed his eyes to close, his mind racing. Part of him in the spirit world? Did that mean he was still in touch with Katsumi Kamo in the spirit world? Was she going to be some sort of personal spirit guide or something, like a weird holiday rep for dead people? For him, the concept of a psychic medium having contact with some all-knowing spirit guide had always been ridiculous and not something he'd ever thought he could sell to clients in his sham shows. It was just too far-fetched. How could one ancient spirit know all the answers to a client's questions and then pass the answers on to a medium? Unless, of course, that spirit was the one and only God. As no spiritual worker he'd ever met was bold enough to claim God was their exclusive spirit guide, he felt on a safe bet that they were all making it up. It always felt suspicious to him that the spirits the mediums claimed they were talking too were from somewhere like Ancient Egypt, Mystic India or a Native American Indian tribe. How the hell 'Assan', or whoever, from Ancient Egypt three thousand years ago knew the deceased 'Bertie Higgins' from the chip shop down the road was at peace now seemed to him simply bloody ludicrous and something he could never convince a client of. He knew the problem for the sceptics, of course, was proving the lie, but he never felt comfortable going down this route in any of his personal readings.

Jade seemed sure that the spirit of Katsumi Kamo had gone for good, so that couldn't be it. In his 'performances' he'd prided himself on using his keen intuition and observational skills, coupled with a few conjuring tricks, to confidently appear to know things about a client's deceased loved ones that he shouldn't. His business was built on the fact that grief at someone's passing was a universal emotion, and his paying customers frantically wanted to believe that their loved ones were safe in an afterlife. He'd built a successful business preying on that grief, providing closure and comfort by pretending to contact their friends and relatives in the spiritual realm. A realm they could never prove existed but desperately wanted to believe in. He knew that the most powerful force in the world was belief. If he could get them to believe in his comforting words, that he was truly in direct contact with the spirit forms of their loved ones, then that would be enough. He knew that when belief is in play there is simply no need for proof.

The ethics of manipulating vulnerable people's belief systems had never bothered him; he'd always justified the deception by the comfort and closure he brought. Now he was beginning to think differently, as if he'd opened a shutter in his soul and let in the supernatural. He felt like he'd somehow been plugged into an electric circuit fuelled with psychic energy, and that power had changed who he was. It was like his brain was tuning into a different frequency on its mental radio, sensing things he'd never felt before. Thinking about it was making his head hurt so he drifted off into blackness again.

By the time he awoke, the late afternoon light was streaming through the window onto his bed and he spotted a yellow envelope that had been placed on his side table.

Curious, he ripped it open to find a 'Get Well Soon' card from Jade with a picture of a beautiful pink orchid on the front. She must have already visited him in the early morning and left him to sleep undisturbed. The handwriting inside was spidery and smudged, suggesting she was having a lot of trouble getting the message down on paper with her damaged hands. It simply said:

Nathen,

I'm sitting here now watching your poor broken face and watching you cry out in pain in your sleep. I don't want to remember you like this – I want us to fill our lives with happy memories and good things, not the pain of the last few days.

Thinking of you.

Love,
Jade

P.S. Lee, Sandra and Kyle say you owe them a beer and a dog biscuit. You decide who gets what.

Then there was a crude drawing of a heart with an arrow through it and a shaky outline of a dog's paw underneath the writing. He clutched the card to his chest and returned in his mind to the hot spring on the mountainside.

CHAPTER 22

TEA AND QUESTIONS

'Welcome to your new nose, Mr Turner,' the consultant said in a matter-of-fact way as he removed the last bloody dressing and held up a hand mirror. He was a middle-aged Indian gentleman with a friendly smile and a name badge that simply stated, 'Mr Kumar'. Another week had gone by and Turner was feeling a lot better, although you couldn't tell from the bruised swollen features that stared back at him in the mirror.

Jade had been to see him most days with the latest news. It was a long trip from Whitby to Leeds and she was helping sort things at the house, as well as handle local police questioning. When she couldn't get there physically they would chat merrily on the telephone, the friendship between them growing stronger each day. Today was a big day – if the consultant gave him the all-clear he could go home.

Mr Kumar pulled down his reading glasses with his forefinger, staring in detail at Turner's puffy features. 'It's healing very nicely,' he said, probing gently around his cheeks, 'and the cheek fracture seems to be doing well,' he continued, using the strange direct tones only reserved for members of the medical profession. Flicking through his charts, the consultant paused occasionally, nodded, turned a page, nodded again and then put the clipboard down. It never ceased to amaze Turner how doctors and nurses never did the one thing a patient really needed – talk to them normally and let them know what was going on. As if to emphasise the point, the consultant was now murmuring to a waiting nurse before remembering his patient was in the room. It just seemed that the job was like solving a puzzle to them and that talking to the puzzle itself was a waste of their time. 'That's fine, Mr Turner. You can go home this afternoon.' Then a bustling entourage of junior doctors, who had been waiting patiently for him to pass his verdict, whisked him out of the room in his smart black suit and shiny shoes.

Jade arrived just after lunch. Turner had been dressed, in eager anticipation, for hours in a navy-blue cactus pattern shirt, jeans and his singed boots. He hugged her closely to him when she'd taken just half a step inside the door and could feel her squeezing him back. She kissed him gently on his swollen nose and smiled into his battered features. 'Hello, handsome,' she said, grabbing his bag and trotting down the corridor. 'Let's go; this place depresses me.' He chased after her, feeling a huge wave of relief at leaving his white sanitised prison.

When they got to the car park, Kyle was sitting impatiently on the back seat of the red Mini, his nose pressed wetly against the glass. Turner stroked him gently, looking into his eyes, wondering if the hairy mutt sensed how close to death he'd been. He decided to sit in the back with the dog, and Jade watched as the two companions snuggled together and fell asleep with the gentle motion of the car. It was a fine day and the radio kept Jade company for the rest of the trip, occasionally interrupted by a sudden burst of snoring from the back seat that made her laugh.

Lee and Sandra were waiting at the house. Lee had a white

plaster cast covering his right hand and wrist and Sandra's left arm was in a navy-blue stretchy foam sling. The four of them looked like extras from a TV hospital drama series as they traded happy greetings in the kitchen, Lee pouring strong cups of tea for them all with his good hand. The kitchen table had been replaced by a white oak affair with four high-backed chairs, and upstairs the lounge had been completely redecorated in pale-blue wallpaper that lightened the room and made it feel warm and homely. Turner did not need to ask why and was thrilled with the changes. Hopefully, the house makeover would be enough of a change to minimise the haunting memories that lived in those rooms. Lee's cast was covered in obscene messages and drawings from his friends, scrawled in blue, red and black pen, and he was vainly trying to hide the worst of them from the girls.

The two men sat and listened intently as Jade and Sandra explained what had happened when the two of them had lost consciousness. Lee had heard it all before over the last couple of weeks but was still struggling to comprehend that evening. From Katsumi Kamo's reappearance and her role in saving them, they moved on to the more grisly details. Apparently, after Stewart had essentially disintegrated into lumps of ash before her eyes, Jade had freed the tape binding the two girls before using towels from the bathroom to contain the bleeding from her hands. Then she had called the police, becoming slightly flustered when they'd asked her the nature of the incident. She'd blurted out 'robbery' as the first thing that came to her mind. Panda cars and ambulances were dutifully summoned and arrived within ten minutes. On viewing the scene in the lounge, the attending police constable immediately diagnosed it as a violent break-in gone horribly wrong, supporting Jade's statement. She and Sandra had confirmed the burnt remains were those of the detective as there was very little to positively identify the body. The constable assumed Detective Inspector Stewart had walked in to find the two thugs torturing the housemates and had taken lethal action with the first things he found – the tranquilliser guns. It looked as if some of his shots had missed as two darts were stuck in the wall next to the fireplace above an overturned coffee table. To substantiate his theory that the guns needed reloading after the off-target attempts, he showed his colleagues the remaining refills carelessly left on the floor. They believed the action of having to load the guns again must have allowed at least one of the thugs to grab Stewart. In the ensuing struggle it looked like the policeman's jacket had caught fire from one of the candles on the table. Despite this, they believed he'd bravely managed to shoot both of his assailants before being swamped by the flames. It was all perfectly logical, said the policeman, and he was extremely happy with himself. The wax found mixed with Stewart's remains substantiated the candle theory, and he left the details for the coroner to figure out.

The brutish fisherman Pearson had died immediately at the scene. His alcohol-abused body could not handle the effects of the knockout drug and had essentially shut down. His sadist partner Roby had lasted longer and died in hospital. If it had not been for the severe beating from Stewart's police baton, he would have made it. Massive internal bleeding meant he never regained consciousness.

Lee chimed in with the rest of the story. Apparently, in the days following, all except the hospitalised Turner had been interviewed separately. None had contradicted the policeman's version of events. Katsumi Kamo's student card and the pink torn note were found lying on the floor near the two large men. In truth, Jade had put them there, not knowing what else to do with them, hoping it might bring questions that would ultimately lead to the discovery of Katsumi's remains. Lee had helped the story along by explaining that the men were arguing between themselves about a body buried under the Pavilion. Although he said he had never seen the student card before, he told the officers he suspected it had fallen accidentally from one of the men's pockets after they were shot. It was a tall tale, he knew, but he hoped there was enough doubt in the policemen's minds that they might go along with it, however briefly. Lee then offered to help the police search for the possible corpse using the snippets of information he had apparently overheard before he had fallen unconscious. With his aid they had found Katsumi's grave within two days, and the police were extremely grateful to the injured guitarist. Forensic tests linked the handwriting on the pink note to Stewart and determined it had been written on a harbour master's receipt sheet from the marina. The police were remaining tight-lipped about what they would do with this information and had instructed the housemates not to discuss it with the press. To the detective in charge, this was a completely separate investigation and had no link to the break-in.

Turner was delighted that his friends had kept their supernatural helper, whom he now knew had ultimately saved his life, out of all police enquiries. Slowly, he described Stewart's sordid confession about Katsumi. They agreed to keep this to themselves, hoping the police would pin the story together from the pink note and the coroner's report on her body. Trying to explain what they knew would just get too complicated and possibly lead them to inadvertently talk about their help from beyond the grave. He wondered how many other supernatural police cases had been covered up by well-meaning witnesses trying to protect their place in society.

All afternoon they swapped stories like a mass group-therapy session. As the light began to fade, a loud knock at the door announced the arrival of a smart uniformed police officer wishing to see Turner. A rather drab plain-clothes female detective marched in behind him and shook Turner's hand with an iron grip. Detective Inspector Ruby Robinson was a fifty-something dumpy woman dressed in a black pinstriped long skirt and grey jacket that made her resemble a dark untidy sack of potatoes. She gladly accepted the chair and cup of tea offered by Turner as the uniformed officer remained standing behind her like some sort of bodyguard. As the others left them to it and retired to the lounge, she flipped open her small black notebook.

'So, Mr Turner, sorry to interrupt your evening, but we do need to ask you a few questions. I understand you were savagely beaten at the hands of these robbers. In fact, I understand you are very lucky to be alive. Had you ever seen these men before?' the detective said, straight to the point, not wanting to waste time.

'Yes, they turned up earlier that day at my door, asking to come in. Fortunately, Lee arrived with Kyle – my dog – when they were outside. The sight of Kyle seemed to scare them off and they left. I have no idea who they are.' Turner slurped at a cup of jasmine tea and stared her straight in the eye.

'And you have no idea what they wanted?' she said, meeting his gaze, raising an eyebrow as she asked the follow-up question.

'No. Just to come in and talk to us about some proposition or other, which I obviously refused. I just assumed they were trying to doorstep me and sell me something,' he replied, still staring straight at her, unblinking.

'Jenkins, who were these men?' she asked, turning to the police constable behind her.

'One worked in the harbour master's office and the other on the boats, ma'am. They have a reputation for violence and petty crime but nothing like this. I think Detective Inspector Stewart handled a few of their cases, if I remember right.' The tall uniformed officer looked pleased with his information.

'Sounds like they probably had an axe to grind with Stewart – he was definitely wrong place, wrong time on this one. Can you remember anything else that may help us, Mr Turner?' Now she spoke more gently, as if she'd established the key facts in her mind.

'I'm really sorry – I was unconscious for most of the time. They were beating me, asking about my possessions. That's pretty much all I remember.' All this was true, of course; he just didn't say which possessions.

Jade came down the stairs, checking he was coping with the questioning, and the detective waved her to join them. She sat down and reached for Turner's hand under the table.

The rotund detective turned to Jade. 'I understand you witnessed the beating of Mr Turner. Is there anything you can add?'

'I don't know what Nathen's said already, but basically they

190

bound him and hurt him trying to find out about things of value in the house. Then he passed out and didn't wake up again. I actually believed he was dead – he was so still and covered in blood.' She gripped his hand tighter as she spoke. 'Then the policeman, Stewart I think you call him, burst in and all hell broke loose. I closed my eyes, I was so frightened. Next thing I knew he was on fire, and the two thugs were on the floor. It was all I could do to free my hands and get help.'

The detective nodded and then turned behind her to look at the uniformed policeman again. 'Jenkins, did you bring the file?' He quickly pushed a brown manila folder into her outstretched hand. Flicking through the various statements and scene-of-crime photographs, she looked up at Jade and Turner, satisfied that their story was consistent with the evidence she already had. As she was closing the file, her mobile rang.

'This is Robinson ... yes ... you've spoken to them ... oh ... I understand. Well, there's nothing we can do so pass the remains to the morgue for disposal ... I know they're bloody shut now ... do it tomorrow. I haven't got a budget for things like this. OK ... bye.' Then she put the phone back in her pocket, looking slightly downhearted.

Without thinking, Jade asked, 'Are you OK?' forgetting she was talking to a police officer. Detective Inspector Robinson was taken aback at the personal nature of the question. The public usually couldn't give a damn how the police felt about things, in her experience. The police were there to solve the crime, carry the blame and carry on, as her old boss used to tell her frequently.

'Well, honestly ... no, I'm bloody well not. That body we

found – the one under the cliffs. The girl ... you know the one, right? You must do 'cos your friend helped us find her. Anyway, we've finally positively identified her after a week of legwork and got in touch with her parents to come and collect the cremated remains. The only problem is, her parents are now very elderly and live in sodding Japan. No offence meant.' She nodded her head at Jade. 'They say they are too ill and infirm to travel the distance to the UK so can we bring the girl's ashes to them? I can't, I mean it's bloody impossible with our resources. Now that poor murdered child is going to be thrown into an unmarked grave with all the other unidentified human scum – the druggies, gangsters, and paedophiles – it shouldn't happen. It's just plain wrong!' She looked a little embarrassed at the unprofessionalism of her emotional outburst.

Jade sat back in thought for a moment. 'Where do they live?'

'I'm not really supposed to tell you, but maybe you've heard of it. It's near a place called Kurama, or something like that. Apparently, it is not far from Kyoto, wherever the hell that is. Why?'

'Yes, I know it.' She glanced at Turner, who was trying to see where she was going with this. 'Look ... why don't we take her back home?'

Robinson shuffled papers, said a polite 'no', and was heading for the door.

Jade followed her. 'I can't let you put her in an unmarked grave. It's against everything I value. No Japanese would allow that. It would be an unforgivable sin in our culture to do this. No – you must not let this happen.' Jade was positively angry now and Turner could see the fire in her eyes. 'Please listen to me ... why don't you ask permission from the family? Give them our names and details and say we'd be willing to make the trip. I know it's not official but, if the family agree, would it be possible? I work for one of the airlines – I can fund the flights with the air miles I'm owed. I'd have to check to be sure, but I'm pretty sure I can sort it out.' Her words were tumbling out fast, pleading with the detective.

'You know, a holiday to Japan sounds good to me right now. Why the hell not!' Turner chimed in, Jade's reckless spirit rubbing off on him. 'Well, Inspector, would we be allowed to do it? I can't work for a while and I'd do anything to keep away from this house for a little longer.'

Robinson looked at the pair of them standing hand in hand, their puppy-dog eyes imploring her to help. 'Maybe if the family gave permission ... I don't know, it's very irregular.' She picked up her mobile and made a call. 'Diane ... its Robinson again. Look, hold off on sending the remains anywhere ... keep them in the lockup for now. I've got an idea, but I need to clear it with the chief. OK, thanks ... bye.'

She turned back to the psychic and stewardess, respecting the charitable gesture they were suggesting. 'In truth I don't know if you'll be allowed, but I'll do my best to make it happen. Do you have any connection with her at all that you know about?'

'No, but we feel her spirit,' Turner blurted out, putting his hand to his chest where Katsumi's spectral hand had touched him. He couldn't help cracking the insider joke and was feeling in much better spirits now that he sensed it was all over. Jade had to hold back a giggle at his remark and Detective Inspector Robinson just assumed the pair of them were of the do-good, happy-clappy hippy type.

As she left, she told them her superior needed to review Turner's statement and if all seemed in order the case would be closed. In her mind, it already was and they wouldn't need to interview them again. Promising to be in touch in the morning about the remains, she left, dragging the uniformed officer behind her.

Jade tugged at Turner's arm, forcing him to bend down close to see what she had pulled from her pocket. It was the ivory netsuke of the mask seller. She pointed excitedly to the feet of the figure where the amber twisted mask of Katsumi Kamo had been. Now there was no sign of the grotesque object. Instead, there was a beautiful white carving of a girl's face and it was smiling happily at the pair of them.

CHAPTER 23

TURNING JAPANESE

Thanks to Lee, the house had a party atmosphere that night. The constant police visits during the last week or so had meant he'd had little time to unwind. He was making up for it now, blissfully puffing on a cigar in the lounge and washing away his cares with a waterfall of whisky. Sandra was keeping pace with a constant flow of White Russian cocktails while Turner and Jade talked downstairs.

During Turner's hospital stay Jade had taken over his bedroom and they were now rather awkwardly trying to sort out the best sleeping arrangements. He offered to sleep in the lounge but she wouldn't hear of it, assuming quite correctly that spending his first night back at the house in the exact location he'd been tortured was not a good idea. Plus his face was still very sore, and he had been advised to sleep on his back for the next few weeks. After fifteen minutes of polite discussion, they agreed to share his bedroom and that Jade would camp out on the floor. She insisted that he had the bed and he felt very unchivalrous as he reluctantly agreed. Turner longed for a more physical relationship with her but wanted to move at her pace. She was totally different to any other woman he'd ever met and he didn't want to mess things up before they'd even had a chance to get started. They grabbed a bottle of wine, and a selection of cheese and biscuits, and headed upstairs.

Through the lounge door they could see Lee laughing as he tried to strum an acoustic guitar with his potted hand while singing a bawdy love song to Sandra. The bittersweet smell of the cigar smoke wafting from the room was overpowering so they closed the door quietly and kept on walking. It wasn't exactly the healthiest atmosphere in which to consume their late-night snack.

They sat on Turner's bed, munching at the strong cheese and toasting each other's health with the wine. In truth, he was glad to be alive.

'Jade, you always seem like a free spirit, living in the moment. I've never been able to be like that. Sometimes I am, but other times the mundane things of life seem to drag me back.' The experiences of the last few weeks had changed him, made him question things about himself he'd never thought of before. Slowly he was trying to come to terms with how he'd lived his life and what direction it should now take.

She reached out and kissed him gently on the cheek. 'In Japan we believe in "Ichi" – the now. We have so many natural disasters – tsunami, floods, earthquakes, typhoons, and even erupting volcanoes – that there is a constant feeling of living on the edge. So part of who I am comes from my culture.'

'Were you always like this? I mean, everybody has a dark side, right? You can't have been so "live in the moment" all your life.' He was keen to learn more about this beautiful lady's philosophy of life.

'As far as I can remember, yes I have. I lost my mother when I was only young and it sort of put things in perspective and made me grateful for my life, really. My father and grandparents pretty much brought me up. It was a very male "get on with it" environment and I guess it just stayed with me. I think moving to America when I was eight just stoked the fire – the original land of opportunity – yeah, right. Everyone is like "go, go, go" over there and they measure success by how much money and things you collect in life. I didn't like that side at all. Anyway, how come you're feeling so melancholy all of a sudden?'

Turner took a deep slug of his wine. 'I don't know. I've spent most of my life wondering what it would be like to fit in – just to be accepted for who you are, without people wanting you to change into something else. I grew up in the North East and we spent a lot of weekends at the coast at a place called Whitley Bay ...'

'Whitley what?' she said, laughing. 'What sort of a name is that? Sounds like something from a pirate movie!'

He was laughing with her, the two of them talking like old friends. 'It's a great place. There's a lighthouse on this rocky island – it was fantastic to explore and even swim if you could stand the cold. We'd walk down the sea front, feeling the freshness of the salt spray on our faces. I used to stuff myself with chips and ice cream from the food stalls ...'

Jade pointed up at his face, giggling happily as he pushed more biscuits into his mouth, spilling crumbs onto the bed as he talked. 'The stuffing yourself part hasn't changed!'

Turner was lost in his memories and missed the joke. 'We were a really close family back then and when I lost both my grandparents in the same year it just broke my heart. I was in my early teens and I couldn't control my emotions – all the kids just made fun of my grief, you know, like kids do.' She nodded, knowing from first-hand experience how cruel kids could be to each other.

'The weird thing was that the first time we went back without them, I saw my dead grandparents holding hands and walking on the beach, just as plain as you are now. It's like they wanted me to know they were happy. I told my mum and dad, and they just laughed at me, saying the spirit world was a big marketing scam, and I was just seeing things. But I definitely saw them plain as day. Nothing like that happened again all the other times we went back so I just thought I'd got it wrong and my parents were right.'

'How can you say that when you work as a psychic? You must have some belief, surely. Things like that must happen to you all the time.' Jade looked at him incredulously, thinking this was all part and parcel of his day job.

'The thing is, I pretended I could see these things with my clients; it was all a big act. At the beginning, I used to believe there might be something different about me but not any more. I remember using those fortune-telling machines in the arcades. You know, the ones with a guy in a turban – you put your money in and it gives you a little yellow card predicting your future?'

She nodded. 'Surely do, but it didn't do Tom Hanks any good, did it?' she said, referring to the movie *Big* where the main character used one with dire (and funny) consequences.

'Yes, that's the kind of thing.' He was laughing with her. 'Anyway, it fascinated me. I used to go again and again and every time I got a different card. It made no sense – I thought it would just keep kicking out the same one for everyone. Plus, each of the cards was spot on – it was like the machine had connected with what was happening in my life at that time.

My friends had tried it and they got an identical card quite a few times. Never happened to me – it was then I felt different somehow.' The old memory was making him think that maybe he'd always been a little different but never really appreciated how much.

He hungrily munched through another biscuit before continuing, 'So when I was older I went to see a seaside fortune teller. You know the type – big board outside saying things like "This lady will help and advise on all things" and "Guard yourself, see her at once". They usually claim to be descendants of Gypsy Rose Lee ...'

'Or Moll Pitcher – we have them in America just the same,' she said, nodding, getting into his childhood tale.

'I went in and there was this young Spanish-looking beauty, no more than thirty, I would say. She was wearing a patterned headscarf and a loose, almost see-through, white cotton dress. To a hormonal teenager, it was enough to make your head spin!' In his mind he pictured the girl as though it was yesterday. 'I put my hands around this huge crystal ball on the table, and she asked me to breathe deeply and gaze into it for a few minutes. Then she picked it up and started telling me things. Private things nobody could know. I was totally freaked out.'

Jade was nodding. She knew exactly what he meant; the same feelings had happened to her when one of her friends had hosted a tarot card evening back in Austin.

'Right then and there, I knew it was what I wanted to do. My dad was like "come work on the boat and earn some cash" – no ambitions for me at all outside of his own experience. He'd spent his life working on a fishing boat with his best pal and couldn't understand why I didn't want to join him. You see, I wasn't very good at school and left with nothing. Determined not to be bullied into being a fisherman I went away and studied – palm reading, tarot cards, and the crystal ball – anything I could. The strange thing was, when I tried it out on my friends, I just found it was something I was good at naturally. But I never believed I had a secret power or anything; I just seemed to be able to sense things about them. It was like I was outside myself looking in and saying things that came into my head. I almost felt as if it wasn't me doing it – more like I was an actor playing a role. As I got more experience, I picked up a few tricks and lies I could throw in that got really amazing reactions. So I kept doing them, and the money poured in. When my dad died I tried contacting him in the spirit world but nothing happened. I just lost all faith in it. Faking it is all I've ever really known and I feel so ashamed of the whole thing now – what I've done, how I've exploited people.' Turner hung his head.

'Look, the people you've seen don't feel exploited, do they? In their view you've helped them, so where is the harm?' She was squeezing his hand tightly now.

'Inside me,' he said simply.

The combination of the alcohol and the strong painkillers were making Turner feel very woozy and light-headed. Jade laid him gently on the bed and kissed his forehead, and he was soon fast asleep. She pulled together a makeshift bed on the floor using a duvet and seat cushions before gently sliding off into her own world of dreams.

Four days later, they were on a flight from London to Osaka, the nearest international airport to Kyoto, carrying a sealed plain plastic urn containing Katsumi Kamo's remains. Detective Inspector Robinson had duly navigated the red tape, and she'd personally delivered the nondescript container to the house. Jade was already on sick leave with her damaged hands so her time off work wasn't an issue. She had managed to get them business-class seats using her air miles, and they'd stayed at her flat in London the night before take-off. The only difference was that, this time, he slept on the floor.

Their short stay in London had provided Turner with an interesting education. Jade had done her best to tutor him on Japanese etiquette while they stayed at her flat, so he was fully prepared for his first experience as a foreigner on the islands. He felt like he'd been through some sort of bootcamp on their culture.

'The good news for you,' she'd explained patiently, 'is that Japanese people like the English. You're an island nation just like us and in some things we are very similar. But our view on the world is very different. Our culture is driven by respect, nature and a belief in the divine, like, say, the spirit of creation rather than a god figure. We have lots of festivals to celebrate it. Simple things like the blossoming of cherry trees or the changing colours of the leaves in autumn.' He had sat on her bed, scrawling notes in his red pocketbook trying to remember as much as possible.

Things started getting weirder as he learnt detailed points on how to greet a stranger. He had brought a supply of his white personal business cards to use by way of introduction. They role-played the giving and taking of the card – he handing it out face up with one hand and she using two hands to accept it. She'd explained that keeping to these rules allowed complete strangers to treat each other respectfully without knowing anything about the other person. He could never master the art of who bows lowest so she gave up on him in the end.

They'd made their way from Osaka to Katsumi Kamo's parents house on the outskirts of Kurama, about an hour from Kyoto. Turner had never seen such breathtaking scenery before. The entire landscape was dominated by mountains covered head to foot in trees and foliage simply bursting with life. The house was set back on its own about half way up the mountainside and could only be accessed by a narrow tree-lined path. The branches arched above their heads and merged together, making him feel like he was walking inside a huge church chapel. It was cool under the trees, and the only noise came from the calling birds and a babbling brook that ran alongside. The air was so fresh and clean that it made him positively light-headed.

Eventually, the greenery opened up into a gravelled garden area that had an array of bright yellow, red and blue flowers and a small decorative well with an arched top in the oriental style. Round stones set into the gravel provided a curving path to a raised wooden platform and the sliding rice paper screens that formed the walls of the house. He stepped gingerly onto the stones so as not to disturb the intricate pattern raked into the gravel and made his way forward.

One of the screens slowly slid back, the noise of their footsteps having alerted the occupants to their approach. An old lady and man stood in the opening, dressed in traditional kimono housecoats and tabi socks. Both looked to be in their early seventies and glowing with health. Time had been kind to them – despite the grey hair, the man was lean and muscular, his eyes shining with intelligence. The pattern on his dark-green clothing was of an intricate clamshell design much like one of Turner's shirts back home. Whether it was because of that or the broad smile on the man's face, Turner liked him instinctively. The woman's clothing was of muted pink with a cherry blossom pattern that suited her rosy complexion perfectly. So much for too elderly and infirm to travel, he thought.

Bowing low, Turner held out his card to the man, who accepted it graciously with two hands and beckoned them inside. Jade also bowed but not quite so low, he noticed, and the woman hugged her warmly. Seemed like the traditional etiquette he'd learnt hadn't quite made it up the mountainside.

They carefully removed their shoes and were shown into a small traditional room with tatami mat flooring and a black lacquer table in the middle. Calligraphy scrolls and decorative watercolours hung from the walls and there was a small desk in the corner with paints, an inkpot and various sized brushes. He wondered if the room was put to use manufacturing the beautiful images when not accepting guests. Other than one intricately decorated small terracotta vase holding a delicate red orchid, there was no other furniture in the room.

The three Japanese knelt deftly at the table and Turner tried to follow their example. Unfortunately, the end result looked more like an inebriated spider trying to wedge itself into a tiny crevice as his long legs splayed out and knees crashed hard against the low surface, causing great amusement to his hosts. Slowly, the older man pulled out a brown leather-bound book from inside the folds of his kimono and laid it on the table with a gentle bow. This seemed like a treasured family possession so, not knowing what else to do, Turner bowed back. The book looked to be custom-made by a fine craftsman, and he guessed it was at least fifty or sixty years old. Strips of light staining streaked the spine and rippled across the front cover. Almost reverently, the man opened the leather volume to show a black and white image of Katsumi Kamo filling the front page. She was smiling happily, and he guessed the black kanji script underneath spelt out her name in Japanese.

'Katsumi,' he said, pointing at the image, and bowed his head again.

'Yes, she is beautiful,' said Turner, bowing back, and Jade translated. Jade reached into her backpack and gently removed the plain plastic urn, passing it carefully to the elderly lady, who bowed deeply and took it into an adjoining room. No one talked until she returned.

The man turned the page of the book, displaying more black and white images of Katsumi. The first ones showed her in a traditional school uniform; then there was a series of her dressed as a goth, probably from about the age of fourteen.

'Goth. You see – goth. She liked that.' Jade translated as he spoke, and he laughed as if amused by the stark black and lace clothing in the image. He turned the page again and this time she was about sixteen and holding a baby in her arms, both of them dressed in traditional white Japanese wrap-around clothing. In the background of the image was a plain wooden crib with white silk cascading over the brim. The hairs on Turner's arms prickled. He had seen this image before in his dream at the hospital. Except then it was alive and Katsumi was lifting the baby to show him.

'Your other daughter?' Turner asked hesitatingly, pointing

a quivering finger at the picture.

He looked straight at Turner and shook his head. 'No … no … that is Katsumi's daughter. She fell in love very early, and you see the result, yes? She was sixteen and a very wild child. We looked after her baby while she completed high school. Then we thought it best if she got away from the area to complete her studies – too many distractions here; she got mixed up with some bad people. So we sent her to study in England – we thought it would help …' he bowed his head in what looked like shame, tears rolling down his cheeks.

For the first time, Turner realised that this man, her loving father, blamed himself for her death by sending her to England. He began to talk directly to him, the words flowing naturally and honestly, reassuring him that her passing was not his fault. The very bad man who did it had been brought to justice, and he knew Katsumi was at peace now. As Turner talked, Katsumi's father visibly relaxed and turned and smiled to his wife, who affectionately reached her arm around his waist. This was the first time Turner had passed on such sentiments with total sincerity. Normally, he made this stuff up for his clients, but this time he knew without any doubt that he was telling the truth. In this moment, Turner felt cleansed of his past deceptions, free to travel a new path in his life.

'Thank you,' said the old man, bowing again. 'We owe you a debt Mr Turner. Thank you.' Then he turned the page again.

Turner froze. The images had changed from black and white to colour, but that was not what made him stare. The beautiful baby in Katsumi's arms had green eyes.

CHAPTER 24

SNOW ON THE MOUNTAIN

Turner couldn't stop himself, Japanese etiquette or not. He reached over the table and grabbed the book. As he scanned each image, he saw that now the baby girl was older and walking. There was no sign of Katsumi in the images but instead a smart Japanese man aged around twenty seemed to be playing with the toddler. Turner kept turning page after page, losing his grip a couple of times as he raced through them. The child was older now in a school uniform and the man was wearing a pair of clean brown work overalls labelled with the name of a Japanese energy company. The final image was a posed school photograph where the green-eyed child looked around seven years old. The printed caption underneath read 'Emiko Akiyama – Midori High School' in English and kanji script. Below the printed text, someone had written in beautiful sweeping calligraphy one word that flipped Turner's world on its head. It simply read 'Jade'. His head spun trying to make sense of it all in the tense silence that enveloped the room. Emotions rushed through him in a torrent, wave after wave. Shock, betrayal and anger fermented together until he exploded:

'Jade, why didn't you tell me you were her daughter?'

Silence. Jade just looked at the floor.

He was calming now, embarrassed at his furious outburst in a stranger's home. He bowed in way of apology to Katsumi's parents, then almost whispered, 'It's OK – you could have told me.'

'I … I … didn't know how. About three years ago I was on a stop-over in Vegas, waiting for my return flight. I decided to buy a crazy western hat as a silly present for my dad back in London and headed to Skips. Eileen Coates, the lady who co-owns the store with her husband, was helping me out, and we just got talking. We talked of this and that and then she started telling me about this cute English guy who'd helped her contact her dead father. When she showed me your business card and I saw your address, I couldn't believe it. You were from the same place in England we thought my mother disappeared from. Or at least the last place the police said she was seen before she left to go back to her student digs. From then on, I always remembered your name – Eileen said you planned to come back to Vegas sometime so I figured we'd cross paths if it were meant to be. Maybe you'd be able to sense something about her, and we'd finally find out what happened. After years of waiting, you popped up on the local Vegas TV news. You were being interviewed at some psychic conference about how you talk to dead people. Then you showed up on my flight. I knew then it was my karma that we should meet.'

No wonder he'd got her phone number, he thought, his ego deflated. Gone was the illusion now that she fancied him, and he felt used. She could tell what he was thinking just by looking at him.

'Look, I swear I didn't mean any harm. I just thought that if you called me I might get a chance to visit Whitby and look for any clues, or at least get a sense of how she lived. That's why I jumped at the chance when you rang.' Jade was pleading with him to understand her motives.

He thought of all they'd been through. Now he understood why she knew so much about the Kamo Clan and the netsuke. It was her family's heritage.

'But your family name is Akiyama not Kamo according to the photograph,' he said, speaking his thoughts into the room.

'That is my father's name. Katsumi didn't tell him she was pregnant. By the time he found out he had a daughter, she'd already left for England. He looked after me and asked my grandparents for permission to adopt me when she went missing. When his job took him to the States, I went with him and everything I've told you since then is true, I swear,' she said, her eyes searching for his reaction.

Turner remained quiet, and she reached for his arm under the table. 'I do have one more guilty confession. Obviously, my grandparents are not too elderly or ill to travel – I rang them before the police got in touch and told them to refuse to visit England. I was hoping we'd be able to travel instead, and they'd get to meet you. That's why I asked the police to get permission from the parents for us to bring the remains back – I obviously knew they'd say yes. It was a long shot but karma is karma. If it was meant to be it would happen.'

'Why?' Turner's voice softening as he absorbed her words.

Her only answer was to kiss him full on the lips, and he held her to him, not wanting to let go. Turner had spent most of his adult life lying for what he thought was a good cause. Now she had not so much told lies as held things from him for the same reason. He reasoned that it was two sides of the same coin and she was no better or worse than he was.

Her grandparents watched on as the two talked and kissed

and talked again. Jade roughly translated what they had said and her grandmother seemed delighted that the truth had finally come out. She hurried off to make their evening meal and sort out the sleeping arrangements while her grandfather politely excused himself and left them in each other's company.

It was a beautiful evening, and the birds were chirping their goodnight chorus as the four sat down to eat. The meal was a simple but delicious combination of fish, soup and fried vegetables washed down with copious quantities of sake. Exhausted, Turner said his goodnights and headed for the small room they had set aside for him. A simple futon lay on the floor with a couple of pillows and a night light. He undressed, feeling the cool mountain air on his skin, and snuggled under the blankets.

The door to the adjacent room slowly slid open, and the naked figure of Jade came sneaking across the floor with her finger to her lips for him to be quiet. The soft yellow night light highlighted the silhouette of her curving hips as she crawled gently under the sheets. Without a word, they held each other and kissed softly at first then more excitedly as their passion grew. She moved his hands between her thighs and pulled her long limbs over him, feeling his body respond to her smooth touch. He could smell the soft scent of roses and lavender on her skin as she pulled him close into her welcoming embrace.

They made love until the early dawn light filtered through the rice paper screens, filling the room with a soft romantic glow. After a lingering farewell kiss, she quietly sneaked her way back to her room. Her grandparents were liberal people, but she did not want to offend their sense of hospitality by heading to breakfast from Turner's room.

The morning meal was a loud, jolly affair with everyone jabbering at once in Japanese and English. Jade handed her grandfather the netsuke, which he accepted with a deep bow. She had forgotten all about it yesterday and only found it this morning when rummaging about in her bag for fresh clothes. He looked carefully at the carving and a wave of relief passed over his face as he saw the smiling mask of Katsumi at the foot of the figure. He bowed again and reached to shake Turner's hand. Turner accepted the small dry handshake with a warm smile; there was no need for words between them. His expression said everything to Turner.

The mist was rising over the top of the mountains, revealing the snow-capped summits. 'C'mon, Nathen. Let's take a walk. It's beautiful up there – you'll love it,' Jade said, pointing up at the clearing sky. So off they went, arm in arm up the forest trail into the mist. She looked at him affectionately and for the first time seemed to see the man behind the mask – the gentle, caring person she knew him to be but that was never exposed to anyone other than Lee, Kyle and Sandra; the one she'd first seen on the plane helping a complete stranger just because he thought she needed him. It all seemed like years ago now but, in reality, was only over a month.

Turner stopped dead in his tracks. 'Oh my God, this is all my fault. I've been going over and over it in my head. It was me who called Katsumi's spirit back by mistake; it was a simple accident. All the death, all the horror.' He was hanging his head lost in his own mourning.

Jade gazed up at the sorry figure in surprise. 'I don't understand what you mean. Why are you blaming yourself?'

'I used your handkerchief underneath the carved puzzle

box to stop it sliding down a chair in the séance at Oswin Hall. The orange one I found on the plane. I was too embarrassed to tell you that before; I felt like a petty thief or something. Now I understand what has happened.' Jade was still confused and said so.

'Look, we know that a person's spirit can get attached to objects, right? We've had living proof of it with the netsuke! What if we all leave some form of energy, our essence if you like, inside the possessions we value? I think something, some essence of you, was left behind on that orange handkerchief. When I put it under the box holding the netsuke at the séance, the connection must have been strong enough to call your mother from beyond the grave. She must have loved you very much – that's what brought her back.' He stood anxiously watching her reaction.

'Look, Nathen, my mother's spirit came to you for a reason; she knew somehow you could help. I don't think you were ever as fake as you thought.' She pulled him to her, looking directly at him, beautiful green eyes filled with affection for this gentle giant. 'If my mother's spirit was able to find you … I'm sure others will seek you out for help as well.'

He gave an involuntary shudder at the thought of it. 'You really think so?'

'Yes, of course. Things we can't see or sense surround us. You know that, right? Sometimes somebody comes along who acts as a bridge between our material world and the realm of the spirits or "shinzui" as we call them here. Well, if you don't know already, you're one of those people.' Jade stood facing him, holding both his hands in hers.

'But I died. I died and she brought me back … why?'

211

Jade squared up to him, challenging him. 'Don't worry about your death – worry about your life. You've got a second chance now. Take charge of your life and be grateful for it – you are who you are, whether you want to be or not!'

He nodded meekly and they walked on in silence. As they climbed higher it began to snow. The white icy droplets seemed to wake him from his musings. 'You know, Jade, I reckon people are a lot like snowflakes.' He held out his hand and watched the soft fluffy white fragments melt when they touched the warmth of his skin. 'Just like these, see? We're all different and the real problem we all face is learning to fit in – it's not just me; everybody feels like that. Now I know where I fit in. I never knew that until now – makes me feel like I'm not on my own anymore.'

'No, Mr Nathen Turner, you are definitely not on your own,' said Jade, and she pulled him to her and kissed him passionately.

Further up the track the white mist was swirling over the top of the mountain. As it dipped and dived between the rocks, the billowing vapour formed light silhouettes of moving shapes. The wispy outlines twisted and bound together, creating strange ethereal faces – old and young, healthy and sick. The faces stared back at the lovers on the path and whispered quietly, 'We … see … you … Turner … we … see … you.'

Nathen Turner would never be alone again.

ABOUT THE AUTHOR

Andrew Langley started writing professionally over thirty years ago to accompany his work as a photojournalist. In a wide-ranging career that has seen him travel the world, his work has featured in national newspapers/magazines and on television. With the onset of multiple sclerosis, Andrew now lives a more sedentary lifestyle, creating his new adventures on paper. *Mirror on the Soul* is his first Nathen Turner novel.

Nathen Turner returns in **Dark Nights of the Soul.**

To discover more about the Nathen Turner novels, and read news, views and extracts, visit:

www.andrewlangley.co.uk

Lightning Source UK Ltd.
Milton Keynes UK
UKOW02f0612220416

272752UK00002B/40/P